FOLKTALES AND LEGENDS OF THE MIDDLE WEST

EDWARD MCCLELLAND
WITH ILLUSTRATIONS BY DAVID WILSON

FOLKTALES AND LEGENDS OF THE MIDDLE WEST

EDWARD McCLELLAND
WITH ILLUSTRATIONS BY DAVID WILSON

TO MY DAUGHTER
Lark

Belt Publishing
2306 West 17th Street, Suite 4,
Cleveland, OH 44113
www.beltpublishing.com

Cover art and book design by David Wilson

TABLE OF CONTENTS

INTRODUCTION

"Have you ever heard of the hodag?" I asked an old colleague from my newspaper days. We were having this conversation over Leinenkugel's and fried cheese curds at one of the several dozen bars in Hurley, Wisconsin, 200-odd miles northwest of Green Bay.

"What," asked my friend, with the newsman's skepticism, "is a hodag?"

"A hodag," I explained, "is a fanged, scaly creature that once terrorized the North Woods around Rhinelander. They survived by eating white bulldogs, and then only on Sundays."

"Why have I never heard of hodags?" he asked.

"Well, they're extinct. They emerged from the cremated carcasses of abused work oxen. The hodag was the embodiment of all the anger those oxen stored up at their ill treatment by foul-mouthed drovers. Of course, oxen no longer haul logs in the lumber camps, so there are no more hodags."

"That story is made up, right?" my friend said.

"Every story you've ever read is made up," I replied. "Words don't magically appear on paper. Someone has to write them down."

"What I mean," he said, "is that it's not true; it's not something I could print in my newspaper."

"You can print anything in a newspaper if you have a printing press and a barrel of ink. A newspaper in Rhinelander was the first to write about the hodag."

I understood my friend's skepticism. I spent a year as a police reporter in my hometown of Lansing, Michigan, where I was taught never to write anything unless it could be verified by an eyewitness. But after years of researching and traveling around America's Middle West, I have become convinced that the folktales, legends, and ghost stories we tell each other are just as true and relevant as anything I ever wrote in a newspaper. To me, the story of how Babe the Blue Ox's footprints filled with water to become Minnesota's 10,000 lakes is perfectly true—and is frankly more interesting than the "official" version about slowly melting glaciers. Likewise the Huron creation tale, which begins with a woman falling through a hole in the sky, onto the back of a giant turtle. And LaSalle's lost ship, *Le Griffon*, returning as a ghost to haunt Great Lakes sailors. I have no more reason to doubt the truth of that than I do the historical accounts of La-Salle walking from Peoria to Montreal to obtain supplies for a new ship. I didn't witness either event, but I read about them both in books.

I believe almost all stories have some truth in them. Newspapers and history books are good for a certain... statistical accounting of the past, but they tend to be written by people who don't understand the difference between the facts and the truth. What I mean by that is simple: a fundamentalist would say the Bible is both factual and true; an atheist would say it's neither. But a discerning reader understands that while Biblical stories may not be consistent with science, they contain moral lessons that can help him lead a better life. Certainly this is true of the Coyote stories told by the Plains Indians. Coyote, a classic trickster character, is always coming up with schemes to get food from the other animals because he's too lazy to hunt. Usually, he ends up outsmarting himself and getting into more trouble than he was in before. It's a lesson in the dangers of thinking you're too smart to work hard. Likewise the tale of Nain Rouge, who has haunted Detroit for over 300 years, ever since the city's founder, Cadillac, struck him with a cane, ignoring a fortune-teller's warning to treat the little red demon with solicitude. Detroit has suffered mightily as a result of Cadillac's arrogance. Everyone should listen to fortunetellers, no matter how mean or disreputable they may appear. Even French noblemen.

Beyond the moral lessons, these stories contain history lessons as well. Reading about Paul Bunyan, the mythical North Woods logger, or Mike Fink, the Ohio River keelboatman, or Febold Feboldson, the Nebraska pioneer, or Joe Magarac, the Pittsburgh steelworker, will teach you just as much about the people who settled and developed the Middle West as reading *France and England in North America* or watching *The Plow that Broke the Plains*. Maybe more, because these are stories told by lumberjacks, sailors, keelboatmen, steelworkers, and other folks who make the world go round. They're "alternative history," to adapt a contemporary term to my own purposes. They constitute a rich history of the Middle West, as told through its myths and legends, which may be a truer history than any bound by the facts.

I read my friend the story about the hodag, which appears on page 100 of this book. I still don't think he believes it's true. Read it yourself, and see what you think.

Chicago, Illinois
December 2017

How Turtle Helped Create the World

I f you've ever heard North America referred to as "Turtle Island," you already know a little bit about the creation story told by the Iroquois, a confederation of six nations who dominated the eastern Great Lakes before the arrival of the French and the English. According to the Iroquois, the Earth rests on a great turtle whose back was a landing pad for the first woman, who fell into our world from the sky. There are almost as many versions of this tale as there are Iroquois nations; this one was heard among the Mohawk in the early nineteenth century.

There is a world above ours, above the sky, where deer bound through evergreen forests, the rivers and streams flow with trout, and the corn grows without planting, plowing, or even rain. The sun is never dimmed by clouds, and the people know no illness, old age, or death.

Free as they are of material cares, the people in this celestial paradise are not free of jealousy or wrath. The story of our own world begins with a man who was consumed by both. He was wealthy, even for that land of abundance, and he was married to a young woman named Ataentsic, whom he suspected of carrying another man's child. One hot afternoon, he sent his pregnant wife to fetch a dipper of water from the spring. On the way back to the house, Ataentsic offered a drink to a sweaty young lacrosse player. In the jealous husband's mind, this was proof of her infidelity. Enraged, he ordered his servants to uproot a white pine and force his wife into the hole left behind.

The servants pushed Ataentsic in so deep that she broke through the barrier between the upper and lower worlds, and began falling, falling, falling through our sky. As she fell, she grabbed the roots of a strawberry plant and a tobacco plant, so she would have something to eat and comfort her when she landed.

Our world was all water then, so only the aquatic creatures lived in it. A muskrat, who always swam with his head about the surface, was the first to spy the tumbling figure.

"Something is coming from the sky!" he shouted.

A loon flew upward to see what it was, and returned to report that a woman was headed their way. The muskrat and the loon held a council with the beaver, the mink, and the turtle to decide who could support this woman on his back. Everyone volunteered, but only the turtle's shell was broad or sturdy for this creature to stand on.

"We need some earth to provide her a place to land," the muskrat announced. He dove beneath the surface, but returned with empty paws.

"If I go any deeper I will drown," he said.

The beaver dove down a little further, but could not reach the bottom. Finally, the mink tried, and surfaced with a clod of dirt stuck to his claw. He set it on the turtle's shell. From this seed of soil grew the land we know today.

The loon flew upward again, and conducted Ataentsic downward on his back. By the time she landed, that speck of dirt had grown to the size of a human foot, so she could stand with one foot atop the other. Soon, she was able to sit down; a few days later, she was living on an island where streams ran beside red willows. Ataentsic planted her tobacco and strawberry, and these were the world's first crops.

By the time Ataentsic was ready to give birth, the speck of dirt had grown into the continents we know today. She lay down beneath the red willow and delivered a daughter. When she grew to womanhood, this girl was courted by all the animals, who transformed themselves into young men to press their suits. First came the loon. He was tall and handsome, with beautiful feathers, but Ataentsic thought a creature of the air would be flighty and unreliable, and forbade her daughter to marry him. Then came the beaver, but he was a creature of the dirt, living in a lodge made of sticks and always digging in the mud, so he, too, was an unacceptable suitor. Finally, the turtle courted the girl. He was short and hump-backed, but Ataentsic remembered the creature who had given her a place to stand in this world. "Marry this one," she whispered to her daughter.

On their wedding night, after the girl had gone to sleep, the turtle placed crossed arrows on her belly—one tipped with bark, the other with flint. That night, the girl had become pregnant with twin boys. One was born in the natural way, but the other, impatient and envious of seeing his brother emerge first, fought his way out through his mother's armpit, killing her as he came into the world. The twins were raised by their grandmother Ataentsic. The elder was called Thaluhyawuku, or Sky-holder. The younger was called Tawiskalu, or Flint, and his body was made of that hard mineral. Flint hunted with the flint-tipped arrow his father had left him, while Sky-holder's arrow was flimsy bark.

These two brothers filled the world with rivers, plants, and animals. They also filled it with good and evil, happiness and sorrow, plenty and hunger. Sky-holder created the game animals: deer, bison, elk, moose. Flint hunted the animals and confined them in a cave. When Sky-holder discovered the cave and set the animals free, Flint created the wolf and the cougar to eat them. Flint placed bones in fish and thorns on berries. He added winter to the seasons, but Sky-holder ensured that the animals would wake from their hibernations and the trees would bud again, so spring would follow.

Finally, Sky-holder made a man and a woman out of red clay.

"The Earth and all that is in it is yours," he told the first people. "Go, and raise a family."

Flint tried to make his own people out of clay, but his first effort had a tail and became the monkey. His second effort had no tail and became the ape. At last, he made a man and a woman out of white sea foam, a fair race that was sent to live on the other side of the ocean.

There was another source of dissension between the twins: Sky-holder's bark arrow could only kill birds, and Flint only shared the animals killed by his arrow with Ataentsic. Because he brought his grandmother game, she came to favor her younger grandson.

One day, Sky-holder was hunting birds by the lakeshore. His bark-tipped arrow, which had always flown true, missed its target and fell into the water. To retrieve it, he swam to the bottom of the lake where, to his surprise, he found himself in the home of his father, the turtle.

"My son," the turtle said, "I have seen how you struggle with your brother, and his designs to hold back you and the people you have created. I am your father, and I will show you how to overcome him."

The turtle handed Sky-holder an ear of maize, the food that would become the staple of the human race.

"Take this and plant it," he said. "It will allow the people to feed themselves when the hunt fails. Your brother treats you badly now, but his wickedness will grow worse. You must kill him, so he can place no more obstacles in the people's way. Gather all the flint and buck's horns you can find: only these are hard enough to pierce his skin."

Back on land, Sky-holder set out to hunt in the forest. When he was returning to his hut, he heard a voice call his mother's name. It was a fawn. Sky-holder followed the fawn until autumn, and gathered its shed horns. For seven years he tracked the fawn, until it was a strong buck with a ten-point rack. He also collected flint stones wherever he traveled, hiding them in a hole in his hut, which he covered with a reed mat. When he was fully prepared to battle with his evil twin, Sky-holder cooked Flint a heavy meal of venison, maize, squash, and beans. The meal was so filling that when Flint finished it, he repaired to his hut for a nap. Once Flint was asleep, Sky-holder built a fire outside his door. The heat caused the stones on Flint's body to expand and burst off in scales. Flint raced to the swamp, to cool himself and collect bulrushes, which he knew were the only substance that could hurt Sky-holder. They battled all night, and all the next day, but Sky-holder was so well provisioned with flint and buck horns that he prevailed.

Since Flint was descended from the gods and could not be killed, Sky-holder threw him over the edge of the world. He now rules the night and the underworld, and whenever he is angry, volcanoes erupt.

NANABOZHO: THE OJIBWAY SUPERHERO

 his tale might be familiar to you if you've read *The Song of Hiawatha* by Henry Wadsworth Longfellow. Longfellow set to poetry *The Algic Researches*, a book of Ojibway legends collected by Henry Rowe Schoolcraft, an Indian agent who operated in the Upper Peninsula of Michigan in the 1820s and was married to an Ojibway woman. Longfellow's title character was based on the Ojibway demigod Nanabozho, who lived around Lake Superior. The name Hiawatha came from the legendary founder of the Iroquois Confederacy, who lived around Lake Erie. Longfellow thought "Nanabozho" and "Hiawatha" were two names for the same person, and apparently he judged the latter to sound more musical. This is a story of the Ojibway superhero, told under his real name.

Nanabozho grew up in the lodge of his grandmother, Nokomis, who lived between the water of Kitchi-gami, greatest of the Great Lakes, and the prairie where the wild rice grows. Nanabozho was different from other children: He could speak to the loon and the moose, and he could take on the shape of the beaver or the oak tree. But Nanabozho was also different because he had no mother or father. When he reached manhood, he asked his grandmother about his parents.

"Nanabozho," she told him, "you are a young man, and you were born to live among people, but your ancestors are not of the Earth. I am a daughter of the moon. Soon after I was married, a rival who was envious of my husband lured me to a grapevine swing on the shore of a lake and pushed me out over the water. I fell through and landed here on the Earth, where I gave birth to your mother, Wenonah. I warned her always to be on guard against the West Wind, Mudjikeewis, and never let it take her unawares. But one day she stooped to pick an orchid, and the wind blew off her robe. In a single instant, Mudjikeewis began your life and ended your mother's. I found you in the woods, on the spot where your mother had last stood. You were less than a baby even, and from that I raised you."

After hearing this story, Nanabozho determined to confront his father, Mudjikeewis. Strong enough to stalk deer for days without rest or to paddle a canoe the breadth of the lake, the young man was ready to undertake his first quest. Mudjikeewis had obtained his power when he and his nine brothers overcame the Mammoth Bear and stole from him the sacred belt of wampum. As a spoil of that conquest, Mudjikeewis became Father of Winds. For himself, he took control of the West, the strongest wind. To the sons of his wife, he gave the North, the South, and the East. But to Nanabozho, his illegitimate offspring, Mudjikeewis had given nothing.

Mudjikeewis lived atop a mountain far to the west, but Nanabozho could cover an acre with every stride. A few mornings after beginning his journey, he came face to face with his father on the peak. Mudjikeewis seemed pleased to meet his son and had no reason to suspect Nanabozho's hostility. They talked for many days, during which Nanabozho got his father to admit he had caused Wenonah's death. After hearing this, Nanabozho decided to punish the old man.

When Nanabozho felt he had fully gained his father's trust, Nanabozho asked his father, "What do you fear most?"

"Nothing!" Mudjikeewis bellowed, standing and puffing out his chest.

"There must be something, Father," Nanabozho said. "No one is fearless, or immune from harm."

Mudjikeewis felt he owed the truth to his son, so he finally admitted, "There is a black stone that would hurt me badly if it touches my body."

Mudjikeewis asked his son the same question. Since his father had confessed, Nanabozho felt honor-bound to do the same, and admitted it was the root of the bulrush.

"I will find the black rock," Nanabozho said, standing up.

"If you do," Mudjikeewis rejoined, "I will find the bulrush."

When Nanabozho and Mudjikeewis returned to the mountaintop, each carried a piece of the substance that could wound the other.

Nanabozho struck first, bashing the rock against his father's breast. Father and son fell into combat. Their fight carried them over rivers, lakes, meadows, and mountains. As they tussled on Isle Royale, the largest island in Kitchi-gami, Nanabozho smashed the rock against his father's head, breaking off fragments that would form the Greenstone Ridge. By the time they reached the end of the world, Nanabozho had injured his father badly, but Mudjikeewis fought on, lashing Nanabozho's flesh with the bulrush root.

"Nanabozho," Mudjikeewis implored, "you must end this fight. The Father of Winds is immortal. If you stop now, I will give you the power to vanquish manitos and windigos, the monsters that bedevil the people of the Earth. And when you have conquered them, I will give you your birthright: you will share control of the North Wind with your half-brother, Kabibboonocca."

Realizing that he could never kill his father, Nanabozho decided to be satisfied with teaching him a lesson, and with a chance to earn a rightful share of his inheritance. When the young man returned to his grandmother's lodge, she healed the bloody cuts and purple bruises Mudjikeewis had inflicted on him. As she tended him, Nokomis told Nanabozho another story about his ancestry.

"After I fell through the lake, your grandfather followed me to the Earth, in search of myself and your mother. Before he could find us, he was killed by a windigo—Megissogwan, the Pearl Feather."

As she talked, Nokomis touched her thin, brittle white hair.

"When your grandfather was alive," she said, "I always had oil to keep my hair lush and supple; now my hair is falling out."

Nanabozho promised to obtain oil for his grandmother's hair, and to avenge the killing of his grandfather. For each of those quests, he needed a canoe, because his people derived oil from fish, and because the Pearl Feather lived on the opposite shore of Kitchi-gami. He built a canoe from birch bark, binding it with the roots of the tamarack and the larch, sealing the seams with balsam and fir resin. He named the canoe Cheeman, and trained it to respond to his commands. Nanabozho ordered Cheeman to carry him far out into the lake, where dwelled Nahma, the great sturgeon who was King of Fish.

Dropping his cedar bark line into the water, Nanabozho called, "King of Fish, take my bait!"

The King of Fish knew Nanabozho was trying to catch him, so he ordered Maskenozha, the pike, to take the bait. Nanabozho pulled on his line. The weight on the other end was so great that Cheeman's stern tipped toward the sky. This must be the King of Fish! But as his catch neared the surface, Nanabozho saw it was the pike.

"Let go of my line," Nanabozho scolded. "I'm not trying to catch a pike; I'm trying to catch the King of Fish."

The pike obeyed, and once again, Nanabozho called, "King of Fish! Take my bait!"

This time, Nahma took the bait. When Nanabozho pulled the King of Fish to the surface, the creature swallowed both the canoe and the fisherman.

"Blech! I just swallowed Nanabozho!" Nahma exclaimed. "Nanabozho, you're the worst thing I've ever tasted. I'm going to throw you up!"

If Nahma expelled him into the depths of the lake, Nanabozho knew that he would surely drown. Nanabozho tried to push the canoe lengthwise across Nahma's throat, so the fish could not swallow or vomit, but he could not do it by himself. Thankfully, a squirrel had tagged along on this fishing trip without Nanabozho's knowledge. With the squirrel's help, Nanabozho wedged the canoe just right against Nahma's giant jaws. Then he took out his war club and battered Nahma's heart until it stopped beating.

When the King of Fish washed up on the shore, Nanabozho and the squirrel were still trapped inside. However, the giant carcass attracted hungry gulls, who tore the flesh off its ribs until sunlight peeped through. Nanabozho peered out of the opening.

"My younger brothers," he called to the gulls. "Make the hole larger so I can crawl out."

When the gulls finished gorging themselves, Nanabozho and the squirrel slipped through Nahma's ribs. He rewarded the birds with the title Kayosh, or "noble scratchers." The squirrel he named Adjijuma, or "animal tail."

"Grandmother," Nanabozho told Nokomis, back at her lodge, "you can find oil for your hair down at the lakeshore. Take all you need. I will use the rest for my next quest."

When Nanabozho finally paddled to The Pearl Feather's lodge, he saw that it was surrounded by Pigiu-waugumee, or Pitchwater, a gooey, gummy slime that floated atop the water and entrapped anyone who touched it. Nanabozho planned to pass through by rubbing Nahma's oil on his canoe. But the slime itself was guarded by two fire-breathing dragons. Killing them would require a quiver full of arrows. Nanabozho built a bow from maple wood, stringing it with deer sinew, but he had no arrows for his new bow. Only an old fletcher (as arrow makers are called), a friend of Nanabozho's grandmother, knew the craft of arrowheads. So Nanabozho paddled back to the lodge and asked Nokomis to fetch him as many arrowheads as she could carry. While she was gone, Nanabozho told Nokomis, he would dance his war dance in the lodge, but secretly he followed her. He studied how the fletcher pounded flint into sharp and lethal points so he could learn the craft himself. He saw another unfamiliar sight, too: the fletcher's daughter, a slender, long-haired girl named Minnehaha, which means Laughing Water. Nanabozho, who had lived with only his grandmother and the woodland animals for company, felt an unfamiliar fluttering in the pit of his stomach. After he conquered the Pearl Feather, he decided, he would return to the fletcher's lodge to see Minnehaha.

Nanabozho fasted seven days before his quest, purifying his body to win the favor of the spirits. Then he set off again across the lake, commanding

Cheeman to take him to the serpents' lair. As he approached, the serpents recognized him.

"You shall not pass, Nanabozho!" they shouted.

The serpents' tails were as long as the tallest trees in the forest. Their flashing scales were every color on Earth: the blue of the lake, the yellow of the sun, the orange of the autumn leaves. They could not move, but their flames could incinerate a man a hundred paces away. To deceive the serpents, Nanabozho shot arrows between them, as though at a distant target. When they looked to see what he was trying to kill, Nanabozho ordered Cheeman to slip past them. Once he was behind the serpents, he shot them easily, since they could not turn to breathe their fire on him. Then, he rubbed oil on his canoe and glided through the sticky Pigiu-waugumee as though it were the smooth waters of the lake. He beached Cheeman just as the oil ran out, and climbed to the top of the hill where the Pearl Feather lived.

Approaching the Pearl Feather's lodge, Nanabozho shouted, "Surround the manito!" in three distinct voices, so the Pearl Feather would think himself besieged by enemies. When the manito emerged from his lodge to see who was attacking him, Nanabozho began firing arrows at him. But none of the old fletcher's arrowheads could break through the Pearl Feather's wampum armor. The manito chased Nanabozho with a club. When the Pearl Feather aimed a blow at Nanabozho's head, the young man did a back flip and kicked the manito in the teeth. The manito tried striking Nanabozho's feet, but Nanabozho jumped in the air and seized him in a headlock. After an entire day of combat, Nanabozho was exhausted. Only three arrows remained in his quiver. As he was beginning to fear he would meet the same fate as his grandfather, a woodpecker alighted on a nearby branch. The birds had always been Nanabozho's friends and allies.

"Nanabozho," the woodpecker chirped, "shoot your arrows at the lock of hair on the crown of the manito's head. Only there is he vulnerable."

Nanbozho quickly fired his last three arrows at the Pearl Feather's top-knot. The final arrow struck its target. Defeated, the manito collapsed face first in front of his lodge. Nanabozho scalped his grandfather's killer and rubbed the blood on the woodpecker's head, coloring those feathers red forever after.

Cheeman bore his master home. As he approached his grand-mother's lodge, Nanabozho pounded his war drum triumphantly. Nokomis emerged to sing and dance on the shore. Nanabozho showed her the Pearl Feather's scalp. Hearing of Nanabozho's victory over the Pearl Feather, Mudjikeewis kept his promise and allowed his son to share control of the North Wind with Kabiboonacca. But Nanabozho could think only of another prize: Minnehaha. He sought her out and asked her to be his bride. Nokomis threw them a great wedding feast. The guests ate Nahma, the King of Fish, and Maskenozha, the pike. They ate pemmican and venison, bison and wild rice. Nanabozho's friend, Chiababos, serenaded the couple with this song:

"My heart sings to thee when thou art near; like the dancing branches to the wind, in the moon of strawberries.

"Thy smiles cause my troubled heart to be brightened, as the sun makes to look like gold the ripple which the cold wind has created."

Coyote: Trickster of the Great Plains

he Plains Indians told a lot of stories about the animals in their midst. They talked about the mother who told the owls to carry off her bad little girl, about how the turtle has a cracked shell because he was thrown into a fire, about how a little boy lopped off a prairie dog's tail, ensuring that animal would always wag a stub there. But the animal they talked about most was Coyote.

Coyote was the trickster of the Great Plains, always begging, wheedling, and deceiving the other animals into giving him a meal—or into becoming one themselves. The trickster appears in the stories of people all over the world: the Norse had Loki; the slaves of the Southern plantations had Br'er Rabbit. Tricksters use smooth talk and guile to outwit their fellow creatures, with varying degrees of success. In Coyote's case, sometimes his schemes worked out, as when he stole fire from the gods and gave it to the people. Just as often they backfired to great comic effect. The Plains Indians loved to recount Coyote's adventures because they violated all the social taboos that ordinary members of the tribe had to follow. Here are a few I can tell you.

I'll start with a story in which Coyote comes off looking clever. One afternoon, Coyote was walking down a hill and saw a gaggle of turkeys. His mouth watered, and he tried to think of a way to put the turkeys in a vulnerable position. So he offered to teach them a new dance. To instruct them, he sang this song:

Lift your necks high, then low/ Wave your tails, to and fro

Turkeys aren't very bright, so they followed Coyote's instructions. When the turkeys lifted their necks, Coyote bit them, and took the birds home to cook for his wife and children.

Just as often, though, Coyote was not as clever as he thought, and his tricks got him into trouble with animals more intelligent than himself. When Coyote was feeling too lazy to hunt his own meat, he stuck a thorn in his paw, and showed it to a raven.

"Raven," Coyote said, "I am hungry, but I stepped on a thorn and my paw is so tender I cannot run after the antelope."

Like all the animals, the raven was suspicious of Coyote, but took pity when Coyote showed him the thorn. The raven fired an arrow into the sky, which landed in his wing. When the raven pulled it out, there was a fatty chunk of buffalo meat on the tip, and he shared this bounty with Coyote. Coyote marveled at this trick. When the raven wasn't looking, Coyote stole his bow and shot another arrow into the sky. The arrow landed in Coyote's thigh, and he ran away screaming until he had the sense to pull it out, finding only his own flesh and blood there.

And then there was the time Coyote spotted a rabbit and chased after him. Coyote hoped to eat the rabbit, but his prey escaped into a hole.

"Rabbit, I am going to cook you and eat you," Coyote shouted into the hole. "I'll throw milkweeds in there and set them on fire to smoke you out. By the time you come out, you will be a delicious meal."

"I'll simply eat the milkweeds," the rabbit said.

"Then I'll throw sunflowers in there," Coyote threatened.

"I love sunflowers," the rabbit said. "I'll eat them and spit the seeds back at you."

"Very well. I will throw pinecones in there."

The rabbit was silent for a moment. "Pinecones are too hard and scaly to eat. Please don't throw pinecones in my hole. Pinecones will kill me."

So Coyote gathered all the pinecones he could find and carried them back to the rabbit's hole. He stuffed them in the opening, set them ablaze, and blew on the flames.

"I am dying," the rabbit wheezed. "If you blow any harder, the smoke will suffocate me!"

Coyote put his snout to the hole to fan the flames. Just then, the rabbit turned and kicked the burning pinecones out of the hole with his long legs. Coyote's fur burst into flames. He ran for miles until he found a stream to douse the fire.

One of the most famous Coyote stories, one told by tribes all over the Plains, is about how Coyote talked his way into becoming a buffalo. There came a time when Coyote grew too old and tired to hunt or even to trick other animals into hunting for him. His fur had fallen out, leaving his once-lustrous coat mottled with mange. His teeth were too dull and loose to bite through a bison's hide. His legs were too slow even to chase a prairie chicken. Despondent, he rested on a hillside, wondering how he would ever feed himself again. But then, he saw a young bull eating grass.

"That bull has all the years of his life ahead of him, and grass to eat as far as the eye can see," Coyote thought self-pityingly. "If I were a bull, I would never go hungry again, and I would have many more children."

Coyote walked gingerly down the hill on his sore legs. He approached the bull, who didn't try to run away from such a sorry-looking sight.

"What do you want, Coyote?" the bull asked suspiciously.

"I want to be a young, strong bull like you," Coyote said. "Bison are the most powerful creatures in the world. The people depend on you for everything: food for their fires, clothes for their backs, coverings for their tipis."

"I can change you into the shape of a bison, but I cannot grant you a bison's power," the bull said. "You will still be a coyote inside. If you find me a wallow, I will do this for you."

So Coyote hobbled across the prairie, exhausting his legs, until he found a wallow. The bull told Coyote to stand in it, then ran towards him head down, the point of his horn aimed at Coyote's heart. Coyote leaped aside in fear.

"Coyote, you must stand still," the bull said. "If you run away, I cannot turn you into a bison."

Coyote decided that a quick death by goring was better than a slow death by starvation, so the next time the bull ran at him, he squeezed his eyes shut and didn't move. The moment the horn grazed his chest, he was transformed into a bison.

"Now, you can eat all the grass your belly can hold," the bull said. Then he gave Coyote some tips for inhabiting his new body: "You must graze atop hills, so you can see hunters. Follow the ravines at night, and hide in the weeds. Always keep your nose to the wind, so you can smell people."

The new Coyote-Bison was young and strong again. He spent his days grazing in the sun, but he was lonely because he did not belong to a herd. Another old coyote approached him with a proposition.

"Young bull," the old coyote said. "I am old and starving and would like to eat grass all day like you. If you turn me into a bison like yourself, I will lead you to a herd with only one bull. We will run him off and have all the cows to ourselves."

"I was not always a young bull," Coyote-Bison said. "I was once an old coyote like yourself, but a bison turned me into this. Lead me to the herd, and I will do the same for you."

The old coyote led Coyote-Bison to the top of a hill, and pointed out where the herd was grazing. Coyote-Bison ran at him with his horn, but when he struck the old coyote, he didn't turn him into a bison—he turned himself back into a sick, lame, helpless coyote! He was so angry he snarled at the old coyote until it ran away. Then he sought out the bull again.

"Oh, bull," he explained, "I was so excited to have young, strong legs again that I ran as fast I could. I tripped over a rock and turned into a coyote again. Please turn me back into a bison, or I will surely starve to death."

"Very well," the bull said, "but from now on, you must stay close to me, because only I can turn you back into a buffalo."

For a second time, the bull ran at Coyote in a wallow. Once again he was Coyote-Bison, he joined the bull's herd. The herd was hiding in a ravine when it was spotted by scouts from a nearby village, who ran home and told the hunters they had found enough bison to feed and clothe every man, woman, and child for the winter. The men of the village ambushed the herd, killing every animal except Coyote-Bison, whose youthful legs carried him faster than any of his fellows. The hunters pursued

Coyote-Bison over hills and across ravines until he came to a cliff. Just as the hunters were about to shoot him, Coyote-Bison leapt over the precipice. As he fell, he was transformed back into his old coyote self.

"I have escaped the hunters by becoming a coyote again," he thought to himself. "What hunter wants the meat or the pelt of an old, broken-down coyote? Now I will go see the bull again. He will turn me back into a buffalo, and I will spend many more years happily grazing."

Once the hunters had returned to their village, Coyote hobbled back to the ravine. A journey that had taken an hour on bison legs took a day and a night on lame coyote legs. When he finally found the ravine, nothing remained of the herd—or of his friend the bull—but bones whitening in the sun. The hunters had stripped away all the hides and all the meat, leaving not even a morsel for a hungry old coyote.

The Legend
of the
Sleeping Bear

 f you've been to Leelanau County, in northwestern Michigan, you've no doubt visited the Sleeping Bear Dunes—miles and miles of barren sand with soft, beige cliffs that rise many stories above the beaches of Lake Michigan. The dunes are one of the most remarkable natural features of the Middle West. Walking through them is like traveling across a desert and suddenly discovering an ocean at the end. How did such an extraordinary landscape develop in this isolated corner of the Lower Peninsula? The Odawa, who once occupied this land (and now operate a casino nearby), have a story about it.

A mother bear named Mishe Makwa and her two cubs lived on the western shore of the lake the Ojibway call Michigamme, for "great water." Before the loggers arrived, this country was richly forested with fir, spruce, and pine. Trout, perch, and whitefish swam in the rivers, like a living current.

Mishe Makwa and the cubs were sleeping under a pine tree when lightning struck its highest branches, igniting a forest fire that burned every trunk and branch for miles around. To escape the flames, Mishe

Makwa led her cubs to the beach. But the fire followed them even there, so they plunged into the water and began to swim. They jumped into the lake at one of its narrowest points, but even there, it was sixty miles across. The bear family swam toward the orange sunrise. They were carried by the wind, which always blows out of the west. Their second sunrise illuminated the fringe of forest on the lake's eastern shore. By then, though, the cubs were exhausted. Their paws had been paddling for a day and a half.

"Mother," the oldest cub protested, "I can't swim any farther."

"Courage, my little one," Mishe Makwa said. "Be strong. There is only a short way to go. We can see the land from here."

The cub lifted his head above the waves. Seeing how far he had yet to swim, he lost heart. His arms faltered, and he sank beneath the surface. A few miles later, his brother did the same. Only Mishe Makwa reached land. She crawled ashore, curled up on the beach, and looked out toward the lake.

"Never again will I abandon my children," Mishe Makwa told herself. "I will watch over them forever. Only the end of my life will end my vigil."

Mishe Makwa's declaration of grief and devotion reached the ears of Gitche Manitou, the Great Spirit. To make her vigil easier, he raised an island over the spots where each of the cubs had drowned. The first island became known as South Manitou, the second as North Manitou. Mishe Makwa was unwilling to take her eyes off those islands. She neither moved nor ate, and it was not long before she herself departed the world she found so worthless without her cubs. Seeing her still in that pose of mourning, Gitche Manitou covered her with a blanket of sand. Every year, it deepens, as the west wind blows more grains over the dunes, an ever-growing monument to a mother's love.

Nain Rouge: The Demon Who Haunts Detroit

hen Detroit was founded, all the way back in 1701, it was as French as Montreal or New Orleans. Drive around the city today, and you'll still see streets named for the *habitants* who tilled the strip farms radiating from the Detroit River: St. Antoine, Jos. Campau, Chene, Gratiot (although that one is pronounced GRASH-it by literal-minded English speakers). The most important Frenchman in Detroit's history was the city's father, Antoine Laumet de la Mothe, the sieur du Cadillac. Cadillac is a forgotten figure: his name is known today only as a luxury car brand, and therefore a synonym for swank and quality. But you can't understand the history of Detroit without understanding Cadillac himself. He created a great city, but he also left it with a curse it's still trying to overcome.

Cadillac was a proud man. Born in France, of a wealthy family prominent in the country's politics, he became a lieutenant in King Louis XIV's army at age twenty-one. Soon after, he emigrated to the New World, where he was named commandant of the fur trading post at Michilimackinac, the turtle-shaped island that guards the passage between Lake Huron and Lake Michigan. There, Cadillac nearly came to blows with a Jesuit priest. The priest had scolded the *sieur* for tolerating the ungodly habits of the *courers du bois*, the fur trappers who sought escape from their rough lives in the fort's abundance of brandy and Native girls.

"You ought not to allow drinking at the fort," the Jesuit remonstrated. "It corrupts the Frenchman and the Indians."

"I am only obeying the orders of the court," Cadillac responded. "If the Indians don't get brandy from us, they'll get it from the English, and then they'll trade their furs to the English, too."

"Obey God's law, not man's," replied the priest.

Cadillac, a loyal servant of the king, told the priest that such talk was treasonous and invited him to take it back.

"You give yourself airs that do not belong even to a *seigneur*," the priest said.

At this, Cadillac seized the meddlesome Jesuit's arm, shoved him out of the commandant's office, and told him never to return.

"I confess I almost forgot he was a priest," Cadillac later wrote in a letter, "and felt for a moment like knocking his jaw out of joint."

After five years on that isolated northern island, Cadillac conceived an ambition to found a more important outpost, one that would control access to Lake Huron, Lake Michigan, and Lake Superior and would prevent France's rivals, the English and Iroquois, from traveling west. He had in mind a spot along the channel between Erie and Huron, a place known to the French as *d'Etroit*—The Narrows. There, he would gather the Indians and teach them the French language, so they and their children would become faithful Catholics and subjects of a worldwide French empire.

Cadillac traveled to Paris to present his plan to the colonial minister, Count Pontchartrain. He returned to the New World with a royal grant of fifteen riverfront acres and a commission to found a new colony. On his way back to *d'Etroit*, Cadillac stopped in Quebec, where he was the guest of honor at a banquet in Chateau St. Louis, the many-gabled mansion of New France's governor atop the rock overlooking the St. Lawrence River. As the guests feasted on pheasant and the governor toasted Cadillac with wine from Burgundy, a knock was heard at the dining room door. A servant opened it, and in walked a woman whose hunched back had shriveled her to a height of barely four feet. Her Mediterranean complexion was as swarthy as an Iroquois's. From her habit-like head covering to the tattered hem of her dress, the woman appeared to be a pile of shuffling black rags. A black cat perched on her shoulder, glaring at the diners with mica eyes. The woman was Mere Minique, *La Sorciére*, a fortune-teller summoned by the governor to entertain the party by reading palms.

Mere Minique made her way around the table, correctly deducing an aspect of the character or personal history of Governor Callieres, his wife, and the distinguished chief judge, Monsieur de Champigny. When she reached Cadillac, he put out his hand and told her, "See what you can tell me about the future; I care not for the past."

Mere Minque examined the creases in the adventurer's flesh, roughened by years of paddling on the Lakes.

"You will found a city," the sorceress told Cadillac, "but because you trade brandy to the Natives, it will come to grief. The Natives will besiege it, and it will be taken from France, first by the English, and then by a nation yet uncreated. It will grow to greatness, then return to wilderness."

"And is there anything I can do to avoid this fate?" asked Cadillac, half-amused by what he considered a parlor trick.

"You must check your pride and ambition," Mere Minique counseled, "and you must appease the Nain Rouge."

The Nain Rouge was a red-skinned dwarf who had stowed away on a ship from Normandy, then hidden himself among blankets in a *courer du bois's* canoe, finally emerging at *d'Etroit*, where he haunted the straits. The Natives and the few Frenchmen who paddled through hoped never to see Nain Rouge; the dwarf's appearance was said to be the harbinger of a great calamity, which could only be avoided by placating him with gold coins or rich furs.

After the banquet, Cadillac mocked Mere Minique to his wife: "A man's fortune is determined by his own doings, not by a weather-beaten old woman," he said. Cadillac was a serious man of affairs, and serious men have no time for the nonsense of soothsaying old hags. Perhaps if he had listened to Mere Minique, the history of Detroit would have been happier.

Soon after the banquet, Cadillac left for *d'Etroit*, leading a caravan of twenty-five canoes containing fifty soldiers, fifty artisans, two priests, and all the supplies necessary to build a settlement: axes, hoes, fur traps, anvils, kettles, and pots and pans for cooking and trading to the Natives. The party landed on July 24, 1701. The artisans immediately built a fort, which was named for Pontchartrain, and a church, dedicated to Sainte Anne, mother of Mary, whose feast day was two days after the settlement's founding. As *seigneur* of the new colony, Cadillac cultivated relations with the Indians, inviting them to play lacrosse near the fort, trading them brandy for furs, and encouraging his Frenchmen to marry Native women, in hopes of building a nation loyal to King Louis in the middle of this new continent. He was sometimes resented by the habitants, the humble colonists who farmed the narrow strips of land along the river, because he reserved the largest plot for himself, as was his right by royal charter, and went about in the seigneurial costume of frock coat and high leather boots.

On May Day 1707, Cadillac and his wife were walking home along the riverbank after the maypole celebrations. Passing two poor *habitants*, they overheard this snatch of conversation:

"Our *seigneur* carries himself very high, with his silver plate and fine clothing, while we pay double for everything," one said.

"Things will soon change," the second replied. "The other day, my wife saw the Nain Rouge."

Cadillac's wife gripped his hand anxiously.

"Did you hear that?" she said. "The Nain Rouge! That's the demon the fortune teller in Quebec warned us about."

"Nonsense," Cadillac said dismissively, with the Gallic haughtiness that would bring his class to grief before the century's end. "As I told you then, a man makes his own fortune."

Just then, there appeared out of the darkness a dwarf, with red skin, goat's horns, canines jutting from his jaws at wild angles, and yellow eyes glowing like oil lamps.

"The Nain Rouge!" Madame Cadillac exclaimed.

Without breaking stride, Cadillac brought his cane down on the dwarf's head.

"You are blocking my path, you ugly little devil," he shouted.

"Arrogant Frenchman!" the Nain Rouge roared. "I will haunt your creation from now until it goes the way of Babylon!"

And then the Nain Rouge leapt into the river, making not even a splash as he sank below the surface.

Cadillac left *d'Etroit* in 1710 to become governor of Louisiana and never returned to the straits. Nonetheless, the Nain Rouge never lifted his curse. As a result, Detroit has seen more trouble than most cities. The red dwarf was said to have reappeared in 1763, when English troops attempting to lift the siege of the Odawa chief Pontiac were massacred at Bloody Run—just as the fortune teller prophesied. He was there in 1805, when a fire consumed Detroit, and again seven years later, when an American general surrendered Detroit to the British—the only time an American city has ever been occupied by a foreign army. Nain Rouge's last reported appearance was on the first night of the 1967 riot, which killed 39 people and destroyed 2,000 buildings. Cadillac's great city, which grew to a population of nearly 2 million, is now home to only a third of that.

To ensure that the red demon never again bedevils their city, Detroiters gather in Cass Park on the first Sunday after the vernal equinox for the Marche du Nain Rouge. Wearing masks, so the dwarf won't recognize them and wreak revenge, and riding on Mardi Gras-style floats, they try to sing and dance away the curse.

"If the Nain does appear," say the organizers, "a struggle will ensue as the evil red dwarf taunts revelers, challenging them to join him in Cass Park, where his ultimate plan for the city's demise will be revealed. The epic confrontation will culminate in one decisive moment—when the future of the city hinges on whether the hopes of the gathered Detroiters can overwhelm the Nain Rouge's dastardly plans, or whether the curse of the Nain Rouge manages to hold the city back again."

The moral of this story is that wisdom comes from the most unexpected sources, and that one should always respect demons enough not to strike them with a cane.

THE VOYAGEUR'S BEACON

n the eighteenth and nineteenth centuries, the voyageurs were the middlemen of the intercontinental fur trade. These hardy young French Canadians left Montreal each May in *bateaux*—eight-man birch-bark canoes that were the only craft nimble and versatile enough to traverse the network of rivers and lakes that led to the heart of North America. Their mission: bring back the beaver pelts required for the hats worn by every fashionable man in Paris and London. They carried with them goodies to trade to the Northern tribes: blankets, calico, pins, beads, flour, pork, silver earrings, guns, bullets, and, of course, rum.

Between the spring thaw and the fall freeze, the voyageurs paddled eighteen hours a day, rising at three o'clock each morning and sometimes covering eighty miles before beaching their craft just ahead of the Northern summer's late dusk. On a good day, they might cover even more territory if *La Vielle*, the old woman of the wind, accepted their gift of tobacco sprinkled on the water and rewarded them with a gust that could be captured by blankets employed as makeshift sails. Tobacco was a great sacrifice; voyageurs stopped to smoke so often they measured out distances in "pipes."

At night, the voyageurs restored their energy with corn or dried peas and pork—a meal that earned them the nickname "Pork Eaters"—then slept under the stars, with only their overturned *bateaux* for shelter.

Paddling was the easy part of a voyageur's life. More strenuous was the portage: carrying the *bateaux* and the cargo over the watersheds separating rivers and lakes. At Sault Ste. Marie, the Falls of St. Mary were too steep for canoes to ascend, so the voyageurs unloaded the cargo and packed it into ninety-pound sacks, which they strapped to their foreheads and balanced on their backs. So laden, they were picturesque figures scurrying over the forest trails: short, sturdy men—tall men wouldn't fit in the boats—dressed in red woolen caps, linen shirts, deerskin leggings, breechclouts, and moccasins.

The voyageur led a treacherous life in those days before lighthouses, sonar, global positioning systems, and weather reports. Many drowned when their *bateaux* were swept away by storms or tore their fragile bark shells on craggy rocks. Only one place on the Lakes was safe: Stanard's Point, at the northern tip of Michigan's Upper Peninsula, where a brilliant beacon represented the spot where a shipwrecked voyageur spent his last moments praying that God, the Virgin, and the saints spare his fellow mariners from the shipwreck he had endured.

Our story begins a few weeks before that disaster in a summer early in the nineteenth century, some time after the French had lost control of the Great Lakes country, but before it had been thickly settled by Americans. A train of birch bark canoes was headed westward to Grand Portage, the gathering of fur traders at the northwest corner of Lake Superior. On an early July evening, as the lead *bateaux* put in near the tip of the Keweenaw, a rocky appendage of Michigan's Upper Peninsula, the graying sky was at the balance point between day and night. As the darkness finally isolated this remote landing from even the sun, three voyageurs smoked their clay pipes and talked of Grand Portage. It was the highlight of every year's journey: while the bosses haggled over the price of furs, the voyageurs were free to drink, dance, fiddle, and woo the Native girls. When it was over, they would return to Montreal in fur-laden canoes—home by September, before the ice began to form.

Denis removed his red cap, allowing his dark hair to fan over his cheeks and neck. Voyageurs wore their hair long, as a shield against the mosquitoes that bedeviled the cool, damp summers.

"Last year," he reminisced, "I danced with a girl at one of the nightly galas. She was too young to marry then, but this year, I think she will be ready. I've brought along calico for her mother, a pistol for her father, and rum for both."

"And when you come back next year there will be a little *metis* named Denis *fils* at his mother's breast," said Armand.

"You have no time for romance," Denis taunted. "Only music."

"One often leads to another," Armand replied. "You're anxious because you haven't touched a woman since we left Montreal; I'm anxious because I haven't touched a fiddle."

"They both have the same shape, you know," Denis said.

"And they both produce the most beautiful sounds a man can hear," Armand noted.

The lover and the musician turned to Honore, who had so far been silent.

"And what are you going to do in Grand Portage?" Armand asked.

"I'm going to Mass," he said. "The Jesuits are always there, and I haven't been since Montreal."

"Those meddlesome Black Robes," Denis spat. "Always telling us not to trade liquor to the Indians. You can't go courting without rum."

"Well," Armand said, "you have your Mass and we'll have our women and music. There's something for everyone at Grand Portage."

Despite the exertions of the day, Honore had difficulty sleeping that night. He had not told his companions the real reason he wanted to see a priest. Unlike them, he had a wife and daughter back in Montreal. Like them, he was no more than twenty-one, and felt the same hardships at four months alone in the wilderness. When the boats had stopped at Michilimackinac to re-supply themselves with cornmeal and pemmican, he had lavished gifts on a young girl's parents, just as Denis intended to do at Grand Portage, and now he wanted absolution, for his deception and his dishonor.

The party rose before dawn and reloaded the *bateaux*. Birch bark is an excellent surface for painting, so the lead *bateau* was a colorful vessel. The gunwales were striped red, white and green, the bow emblazoned with the dark specked head of a loon. The name *Trois-Rivieries*—the Quebec village where the boat had been constructed—was lettered on both sides. As the boats neared Keweenaw Point, a treacherous cape where surf smashed against copper-filled ochre rocks, the voyageurs began singing. To keep the paddles in time, and to distract themselves for their drudgery, voyageurs sang of women, of nature, of life in the canoes, of the French motherland most of them had never seen, and never would. That morning, they sang "A La Claire Fontaine." In English, it means "At the Clear Running Fountain." It goes like this:

A la claire fontaine
M'en allant promener
J'ai trouve l'ean si belle
Qui je m'y suis baigne

Lui ya longtemps que je t'aime
Jamais je ne t'oublierai

At the clear running fountain
Sauntering by one day
I found it so compelling
I bathed without delay

Your love long since overcame me
Ever in my heart you'll stay

Keweenaw Point was considered such a navigational hazard that some crews portaged across the peninsula rather than risk its rocky outcroppings. But the men of the *Trois-Rivieres* were in a hurry to reach Grand Portage, and thus not eager to hump their cargo across twenty miles of stony ground.

That morning was so windy that one Denis joked, "Someone must have sacrificed an entire pouch to *La Vielle*."

"Perhaps if we sprinkle some on the water, we can persuade her to calm the winds," Armand suggested.

This he did, but the winds grew stronger and stronger, until not even the exertions of eight men could control *Trois-Riviere's* course. The *bateau* climbed and dove on the swelling waves, until finally its hull smashed into the granite ledge that would later be identified on nautical charts as Stanard's Point. The granite rent such a breach in the boat's bark skin that not even a sponge kept on board could soak up all the water gushing through it. The *Trois-Rivieres* sank, carrying its cargo and crew to the bottom of Lake Superior.

Stanard's Point is almost entirely submerged, except for a shelf of rock just large enough for a man to pace back and forth. Only one member of the *Trois-Riviere's* crew was a strong enough swimmer to attain this refuge: Honore. Finding a handhold on the granite, he lifted himself onto the exposed rock and stood up, even as the waves washed across his waterlogged moccasins. And then he began to do the only thing a shipwrecked mariner can do in this situation: he prayed. To the Father. To the Son. To the Holy Mother. To the Holy Mother's mother, Sainte Anne. To St. Brendan the Navigator, patron saint of sailors. Honore prayed only that he be spared long enough to confess to a priest, so he could ascend to heaven unencumbered by his sins. Perhaps God or a saint would guide another *bateau* in the caravan back to this rock. But none came. Honore was surrounded by all the water he could ever drink, so he didn't go thirsty. He was also surrounded by all the fish he could eat, but he had no way to catch them. A week passed under the July sun. Honore grew weaker and weaker. When he finally passed from hope to resignation, he stopped praying for his own salvation, and prayed instead for the safety of other voyageurs who might pass this spot.

On the journey back from Grand Portage, only one *bateau* full of foolhardy voyageurs decided to risk a trip around Keweenaw Point. The wreck of the *Trois-Rivieres* had turned the rendezvous into a solemn memorial. Instead of dance tunes, the fiddlers played dirges. In addition to performing weddings between Frenchmen and Native girls, the Black Robes said masses for the drowned voyageurs. Almost all the crews agreed that from now on, it would be safer to portage across the Keweenaw, no matter the effort, rather than risk another disaster. The one crew that disagreed argued that the storm, not the rocks, had sunk the *Trois-Rivieres*. As they paddled toward Stanard's Point, they saw a light, bright enough to assert itself on a cloudless noon. Even across miles of water, they could see it formed the shape of a man, with a cap, a sash, a pouch, leather leggings and moccasins.

"Boys, I think we need to steer clear of that beacon," declared the bowsman. The bowsman was the voyageur who guided the craft's progress, and carried it during portages, along with the steersman, who sat in the back.

Never again did a *bateau* or a ship crash against Stanard's Point. The beacon shone for over a century, until a lighthouse was built on the rock where Honore had spent the final days of his life. Then, his service to his fellow mariners completed, his light went out.

MIKE FINK AND THE PIRATES OF THE OHIO

'm the Salt River Roarer!" Mike Fink liked to bellow to any man or woman he met. "I can out-run, out-jump, out-shoot and lick any man in the river. I'm half sea-dog, and the rest of me is Kentucky war horse, Ohio snapping turtle, and Mississippi gator."

Mike Fink was the biggest, toughest, brawlingest, straight-shootingest keelboatman who ever sank a pole into the Ohio or the Mississippi. When Mike bragged—which was whenever he opened his mouth, except when he was pouring whiskey down his throat—he bragged in a voice so deep and loud that a man standing on the Cincinnati docks could hear him from all the way across the river, in Kentucky. Everyone in the Ohio Valley knew about Mike Fink's exploits, and if they didn't, he told them.

"I can shoot a whisker off a sleeping cat at fifty yards without waking him up," he boasted. "I love women and I love a good fight."

Mike was born at Fort Pitt, a few years after the English took it over from the French. In his youth, he was a market hunter, killing deer for the Pittsburgh butchers. Then he was an Indian scout, patrolling the wilderness for threats to the settlement, spending weeks in the woods with no provisions but jerked venison, corn meal, and a rifle for hunting his own meat. The Battle of Fallen Timbers pushed the Indians westward in 1793, so they no longer menaced Pittsburgh, but Mike was by then too wild a character to settle down as a farmer or a merchant. Like other restless men who couldn't stand to live less than a rifle shot from their nearest neighbor, Mike followed the frontier westward, hiring on as a keelboatman on the Ohio and Mississippi rivers, which then formed the edges of American civilization. Rivers were the superhighways of that era. A keelboat—a long, low, wooden vessel with a cabin in the middle of the deck—was the fastest means of carrying a load of cargo from Pittsburgh to New Orleans. To get back upstream, the crew would sink long poles into the mud and walk from bow to stern, outmuscling the current. No one could travel more miles in a day than Mike, who was six feet tall, weighed 180 pounds, and within those dimensions was built like an American Hercules.

When rival boats met on the river, or tied up in the same port, it was customary for the crews to repair to the shore for a good-natured fight, either in a tavern, or, if they'd washed up in a dry county, a clearing in the woods. During those brawls, which sometimes went on for hours, men would have their eyes gouged out, then crawl along the floor to find the missing orbs and pop them back in their sockets, so they could see clearly to continue the battle. The winner of these fights was rewarded with a red turkey feather. No one had more feathers bristling from the band of his beaver hat than Mike Fink.

After an enjoyable afternoon of punching, kicking, and gouging his fellow boatmen, Mike would seek out his favorite refreshment: Kentucky bourbon.

"I can drink a gallon of whiskey in twenty-four hours and still walk a straight line and recite the Declaration of Independence from top to bottom," was another of his boasts.

But not even a man who could hold his whiskey was immune to the corrosive effects of alcohol. Mike drank so much bourbon it ate away the lining of his stomach.

"Unless your stomach grows a new lining," a frontier doctor told him, "you won't be able to drink another drop without killing yourself."

Never drinking another drop sounded worse to Mike than killing himself. So he shot a buffalo, skinned it, and swallowed its wooly hide, which from then on soaked up all the whiskey he drank.

Even beyond his renown as a tippler, Mike was most famous for his shooting. His six-foot-long rifle, Bang-All, was adorned with brass and silver inlays in the shapes of Indians, dogs, hearts, eagles, and a sheriff's star. His best-known trick was shooting a cup of whiskey off a man's head at forty paces, which he would perform for a silver dollar wager.

In the nineteenth century, with the frontier still a living memory, Mike Fink was a household name. He was a hero of dime novels, and showed up as a character in *Davy Crockett's Almanack*, an annual publication that kept the King of the Wild Frontier's name and exploits alive after he was killed at the Alamo. According to the almanac, Mike was the only man ever to outshoot Davy. The Kentucky frontiersman once spent a night with Mike at his cabin on the Cumberland River.

"I've got the handsomest wife, and the fastest horse, and the sharpest shooting in all Kentucky," Mike bragged to Davy. "Do you see that cat sleeping on the top rail of that fence, a hundred and fifty yards yonder? I'll trim its whiskers, and it won't stir a muscle."

Mike's aim was so true that he shot off every whisker without waking the cat.

"You left a half-inch off that last one," Davy pointed out, and shot it off cleanly.

Desperate to outdo the great Davy Crockett, Fink spotted his own handsome wife, Peg, walking to the spring with a gourd to collect water. Raising Bang-All to his shoulder, he shot half the comb off her head. Not a hair stirred, and Peg never looked up.

"Now you shoot off the rest," he challenged Davy.

"Mike, you've got me beat," his guest conceded. "I couldn't hold my hand still if I pointed this rifle anywhere near a woman. Let's have ourselves a dram of whiskey and I'll be on my way."

Mike had to be tough with his fists and sure with a bullet, because in the early nineteenth century, the lawless years before statehood, the lower Ohio River was bedeviled by pirates who would hijack a boat, kidnap or kill its crew, and pilot the trophy downriver to New Orleans, where they sold the cargo for an enormous profit before news of their treachery reached civilization. The pirates' favorite hide out was Cave-in-Rock, a deep, low shelter that looked out on the Ohio from the southern tip of the Illinois Territory. A freebooter named Samuel Mason set up his headquarters there, enticing boatmen ashore with a sign advertising "Liquor Vault and House of Entertainment." If that didn't bring 'em in, Mason dispatched a confederate to pose as a pilot who could guide the boat through the treacherous channel. Instead, the pilot ran it aground near the cave, where Mason and his pirates overwhelmed the gullible crew and looted their cargo. The story of Mike's tangle with the pirates was told in *Mike Fink: Legend of the Ohio*, a dime novel by Emerson Bennett, one of the best-selling authors of the pre-Civil War era. It was also portrayed in the Walt Disney movie *Davy Crockett and the River Pirates*, the one and only time Mike has been portrayed onscreen.

The pirate-infested Lower Ohio was so feared by keelboatmen that when Mike was loading his keelboat, *Light-foot*, at the Cincinnati docks, he and his crew took time out to visit a soothsayer named Mother Deb, "to find out whether we're going to be hanged or drown." The *Light-foot* was carrying a shipment of gold to a bank in St. Louis. Pirates would kill for that kind of plunder.

A ragged crone who lived in a rickety cabin atop one of the Seven Hills overlooking the Ohio, Mother Deb always leaned on a hickory staff with a horseshoe nailed to the head as a defense against witches. Reading from playing cards spread across her wobbly table, Mother Deb forecast a bloody end for Mike Fink. Beware, she warned him, of a heavy, swarthy man with a black beard.

"Even if you survive your coming ordeal, you will have many years and many dangers ahead of you," she told Mike.

"Well, boys, you heard the old woman," Mike addressed his crew as they headed back to the docks. "If you didn't want a little danger, you should have gotten a job in a counting house. I can lick five times my weight in wildcats, so if a little danger keeps me onshore, my name's not Mike Fink!"

Light-foot set out with four passengers, including Aurelia Fontaine, a young woman from Mexico who was seeking to return to Vera Cruz by way of New Orleans. Also on board was a stranger who had paid for passage as far as Shawneetown, a trading post on the north bank of the river in Illinois.

The first trial of any keelboat journey was the Falls of the Ohio, at Louisville, a rapids that carried a boat on a switchback descent, threatening to dash it against the rocks over which the river spilled. Mike stood in the bow of *Light-foot* and guided his crew toward the one safe channel through the Falls.

"Steady, all, steady!" he cried. "Give her the chute, then."

When *Light-foot* was safely past the Falls, and again floating on smooth waters, Mike opened the whiskey keg. The crew drank its daily dram and sang a tune known to all who traveled the river:

"Some rows up, but we floats down
Way down the Ohio to Shawneetown
Haul on the beech oar, she moves too slow
Way down to Shawneetown on the Ohio
I've got a gal in Louisville, a wife in New Orleans
When I get to Shawneetown I'll see my Indian queen.
Now them good ol' boys, they talk loud and long.
They wide as a barrel and their twice as strong
The water's might warm, boys, the air is cold and dank,
And the cursed fog it gets so thick you cannot see the bank.
Now the current's got her and we'll take up the slack.
Float her down to Shawneetown and we'll bushwack her back.
Some rows up, but we floats down,
Way down the Ohio to Shawneetown."

The next afternoon, the stranger got off the boat at Shawneetown — only twenty-five miles upriver from Cave-in-Rock.

"We're going to tie up here for the night," Mike ordered. "I'm not floating past that nest of pirates in the pitch darkness. That's the only way they can win a fight. I'll lick a hundred pirates with my bare hands in broad daylight."

Mike and his men were playing cards below decks when they felt *Light-foot* shake and heard footsteps up above. Mike grabbed a pistol off the wall and raced up the ladder, where he confronted a man dressed in the pirate's costume of red skull cap, black-and-red striped shirt, linsey-woolsey trousers, and leather boots. The stranger wore every accoutrement of the desperado save a gun and a knife hanging from his belt. He held his hands above his head to show he carried neither.

"Who goes there?" Mike demanded.

"Ned Groth," the man replied. "I'm a member of Samuel Mason's gang—or was, until a few hours ago, when I got into a donnybrook with another fella over my share from our last raid. Mason told his henchmen to take me out to the rocks and shoot me, because he didn't want no malcontents in his gang. But I overpowered 'em and threw their guns in the river. Then I jumped in myself."

"And what are you doing on my boat?"

"That fella who got off in Shawneetown was one of Mason's confederates. He let the boss know you got valuable cargo, and there's two boatloads of pirates headed this way right now."

Before Mike could call an alarm to his crew, he heard the sound of oars stirring the water and saw the silhouettes of a pair of rowboats, still far enough away that they were darker than the surface. Mike ran to the head of the ladder and shouted down into the cabin.

"Boys, we got a good old fight coming! Every one of you grab a pistol, because there's two boatloads of pirates a-headed this way!"

When Mike Fink shouted a warning, it could be heard by boats for miles up and down the river. But even before his crew could arm themselves and scramble up the ladder, Mason and his pirates were tumbling over *Light-foot's* gunwales. Mike's first mate, a young man named Fontaine, shot one of the bandits and tossed him in the river. Mason returned fire, putting a bullet through the boy's neck. In the on-deck confusion of gun smoke, fists, and knives, Mason and two fellow pirates slipped down into the cabin. They emerged with all three passengers, holding a gun to each captive's back.

"Now everyone just stop shooting, and this young lady and these two gentlemen won't be harmed," Mason commanded, as he edged across the deck with his prisoners. "And once we get the ransom they're worth, they can continue on their journey."

Mason forced the terrified passengers into a waiting rowboat. Before it began the journey back to Cave-in-Rock, he shouted orders to the pirates still aboard the *Light-foot*.

"Now you boys bring me back the entire boat, and there'll be a reward for everyone."

The fight resumed, but without their leader, the pirates were no match for Mike Fink. With his hairy, callused fist, he hit one pirate so hard the man landed on the rocks in Kentucky, bounced once, and landed again in Tennessee. The wounded and the survivors finally leaped off *Light-foot's* deck and swam frantically back to the rowboat Mason had left them.

"I shook them more than an earthquake," Mike boomed, as he watched the overloaded boat wallow back to Illinois. "I'm stronger than the current of the Mississippi, more dangerous than lightning, and more terrifying than waking up with a wildcat in your bed."

The next morning, after sleeping off a day of drinking and a night of fighting, Mike told his crew that he wanted to attack the pirates' hideout, and that any man who wasn't with him was welcome to swim back to Cincinnati with a yellow stripe on his back.

"We promised to bring them folks to New Orleans, and by God, we will, without paying a penny in ransom to those ragged, skulking river pirates. We'll lick them or die!"   Every man went with Fink. The turn-coat, Ned Groth, explained that the opening to the cave was hidden by rocks, to blend in with the rest of the bank, but that he could lead them to a landward entrance. The cave was likely to be guarded by a dozen pirates, but if they attacked after dark, when the drinking began, they could overcome the watchmen.

At sunset, Mike unmoored *Light-foot*. The current carried it unnoticed past the pirates' lair and up a creek just beyond the cave. Ned Groth led the crew down a woodland path that his boots knew even in the darkness. A hundred yards from the cave, they encountered a sentry.

"It's Ned Groth's ghost!" exclaimed the frightened pirate, unaware that Groth had escaped Mason's death sentence and joined Mike Fink's crew.

Mike pushed past Groth and confronted the man.

"It's not Ned Groth's ghost, it's Ned Groth in the flesh," he boomed, in that voice loud enough to cross rivers. "And I'm Mike Fink in the flesh. If you know what's good for you, you'll step aside and give me back my passengers. Otherwise, my men and I will run you out of this cave like we ran you off my boat."

Mike Fink, God bless him, could never resist an opportunity to boast.

This time, his boasts were an alarm to the pirates, who poured out of the cave with pistols cocked. All except their chieftain, Samuel Mason. Mason was clambering down the rocks with his prisoners, who he forced into a rowboat at the point of a gun.

Once again, Mike Fink's men routed the pirates, in a skirmish that briefly disturbed the dark, silent night with muzzle flashes, explosions of gunpowder, cursing, the crack of man's fist against another man's head, and finally, the terrified wails of the pirates as they scattered into the countryside, where they hid among the trees, each hoping to save his own life. The crew entered the cave, which was filled with the booty from half-a-dozen doomed boats that had been captured or run aground at Cave-in-Rock: barrels of flour and molasses, bags full of hard money, guns, knives, and, of course, casks of whiskey. But no sign of the captives. As the men began searching deeper into the low-ceilinged cave, they heard, from the river, a woman's cry for help. Mike raced onto the rocks, pistol in hand, and saw a rowboat with three figures receding into the gloaming. Few marksmen would dare to take a shot at a moving target in the darkness, especially when there was a risk of hitting an innocent young lady. But Mike Fink never lacked confidence in his shooting. Or anything else, for that matter. He raised the pistol, drew a bead on Samuel Mason, and fired one shot, just before the darkness rendered his quarry invisible. He knew by the sounds of celebration on the boat that the bullet had struck home.

"Come on, boys," he ordered two boatmen standing on the rocks with him. "Let's bring 'em back to shore."

They jumped in the water, swam to the middle of the channel, and rowed the boat back to safety. After that, keelboatmen never had to fear

Cave-in-Rock. With their leader gone, the pirates never returned to the cave, or harassed river traffic.

Instead, the keelboats had a new enemy. In 1807, a man named Robert Fulton designed a boat with a steam engine that turned a paddlewheel. It traveled the 150 miles up the Hudson River from New York City to Albany in just 32 hours. Within a decade of that maiden voyage, steamboats were plying the Ohio and the Mississippi. The first time Mike Fink saw one, on a cold October morning, he thought it was Noah's Ark, and the steam unfurling from its pipe was the breath of every animal God had ordered Noah to gather. Mike came to despise any boat that was powered by a mechanical engine, rather than a strong man's muscles. One day in 1822, *Light-foot* was headed up the Mississippi, just south of St. Louis, when it encountered a steamboat traveling downstream.

"Captain Mike, she wants the channel," the steersman said.

"Well, then let her try for it," Mike growled. "I'll be damned if I yield to any steamboat."

Mike stood in the prow of his beloved boat, staring impassively as the steamboat grew larger and larger in his vision, until the vessels collided with a splintering crash. The steamboat's boiler exploded. Its chimney collapsed. Its wooden planked sides caved in. The crew and passengers leapt overboard, swimming frantically to shore. The crash sank *Light-foot* as well, and Mike found himself stranded in St. Louis, without a boat to command.

The steamboat, he understood, was not only making his livelihood obsolete, it was bringing settlers to the Northwest, and with settlers came civilization—that way of life to which the Salt River Roarer had never been able to reconcile himself. Ohio, Indiana, Illinois, and Missouri had all joined the Union since Mike became a keelboatman. The frontier was moving westward, and Mike felt compelled to follow it. So he became a fur trapper, joining General William Ashby's expedition to the Missouri River country. His marksmanship made him one of the most valuable members of Ashby's company. At Fort William, on the Yellowstone River, Mike purchased a hundred bullets at the commissary, and predicted, "I'll feed the fort all winter with these." With a hundred shots, he killed a hundred bison. The trappers and the Shoshone Indians feasted for weeks, while Mike sold the hides for fifty cents apiece.

But Mike was in his fifties—an advanced age then, especially for one who had led such a rough, vigorous life—and finally his shooting hand and marksman's eye failed him. This had fatal consequences, both for himself and one of his companions. Every year, the trappers threw a frolic to celebrate the arrival of spring, and their release from the snowbound isolation of winter. They drank whiskey, fiddled, danced, and tried to one-up each other by telling the most outrageous tall tales. Of course, Mike had to show off his famous shooting trick.

"Carpenter," he challenged a young man who had wintered out with him in a cave, "I'm going to set a cup of whiskey on my head. I want you to walk off forty paces and see if you can knock it off my head."

Carpenter did so, but his shot grazed Mike's scalp, singeing off a lock of graying hair and bloodying a strip of skin.

"Son, I thought I taught you how to shoot," Mike taunted.

"Well, let's see you do it, old man," Carpenter said, setting a cup on his own head.

Mike paced off the proper distance, turned and raised Bang-All to his shoulder for the final time. He pulled the trigger, and for the first time ever, his shot missed. It struck Carpenter in the forehead, killing him instantly.

It so happened that Carpenter's brother—a swarthy, bearded man—was also on the expedition and had witnessed the shooting contest. Seeing his kin collapse in the dirt, he rushed toward Mike Fink, crying "Murderer!" Mike turned on him, full of rage.

"I was as close to that boy as I am to anyone in this company," Mike shouted. "If you think I put a bullet through him on purpose, why, there'll be a real murder."

And there was. Carpenter's brother pulled two pistols from his belt and fired both into Mike Fink's heart. It was just as the soothsayer in Cincinnati had predicted: after many years, many dangers and many ordeals, Mike Fink had come to a bloody end.

FEBOLD FEBOLDSON: NEBRASKA'S PRAIRIE GENIUS

uring the pioneer days, tens of thousands of prairie schooners—horse-drawn covered wagons—crossed the plains of Nebraska on their westward journey along the Oregon Trail. Most were just passing through. Some were on their way to California, where the rivers ran with gold and the trees dripped with fruit. Others were headed to Oregon, whose lush grasses fattened dairy cows. Very few stopped in Nebraska, a treeless, dusty land nicknamed the Great American Desert.

The Nebraska summers were so hot that birds wouldn't lay their eggs, because they came out poached. The winters were so cold that words froze as soon as they left a man's mouth. They had to be carried inside and thawed out on the stove so people could hear what they'd said to one another. During droughts, the air was so thick with dust that Nebraskans cut it into squares, packed it in boxes, and sold it as fill dirt to landscapers in New York.

Only the most resourceful pioneer could survive in a landscape so harsh, and no pioneer was more resourceful than Swedish immigrant Febold Feboldson. According to his grand-nephew, Bergstrom Stromberg, if Febold had filed all his inventions with the patent office in Washington, DC, he would be remembered as a more prolific tinkerer than Thomas Edison or Henry Ford.

Febold and his cousin Hjalmar sailed to America from Sweden some time between the opening of the Oregon Trail and the beginning of the California Gold Rush. They headed west across the continent, hoping to reach the Pacific Ocean. But in the middle of Nebraska, on a hot, arid summer day, Hjalmar was overcome by homesickness for the cool streams of Scandinavia. In a delirium, he dove headfirst into a muddy trickle of water.

"This is about the most dismal river I've ever seen," Febold remarked, as he pulled his cousin's head out of the silt. It turned out Hjalmar had broken his neck, which would take months to heal, so on the Dismal River they stayed. Their first year in Nebraska, the cousins lived in a "soddie," a hut constructed of chunks of sod, the only building material available in that treeless country. Since they had arrived too late to plant a crop, Febold survived by hunting the mugwump, a bird whose head and tail looked exactly the same. The mugwump itself couldn't tell the difference, and flew around in circles because it didn't know which way it was headed. The bird's confusion made it easy prey, and the settlers hunted it to extinction before Audubon could arrive to paint its portrait, which is why the mugwump is never found in ornithology textbooks.

The fiercest threats to Febold's survival were not the wolves, or the coyotes, or even the Pawnee. No, the fiercest predators on the prairie were the mosquitoes. Prairie mosquitoes were so big they could they could drink all a man's blood even faster than a cowboy could empty a bottle of whiskey. When a flock of mosquitoes attacked his soddie, Febold hid inside an iron boiler he had brought west in his prairie schooner. The mosquitoes stuck their needles through the iron, so Febold bent them with a hammer, making it impossible for the furious insects to pull them out. When the entire flock was trapped, Febold walked outside and sliced their stingers off with a knife, so they could never drink blood again. After that, he covered his soddie with a mosquito net fashioned from four-inch-thick steel cables.

Hjalmar's neck never healed properly. His head was bent at a right angle to his body, which meant Febold had to carry him around sideways so he could see straight. A man can't travel long distances in that condition, so the cousins settled down in Nebraska. Febold thought they deserved a log cabin, like the one they'd left behind in Sweden, so he walked all the way to California, cut down a dozen redwoods, and dragged them back to Nebraska on a logging chain. Febold then raised a two-story cabin and had enough wood left over so that when a ten-foot blizzard fell the next winter, he built a giant plow. Febold harnessed the plow to a herd of buffalo he had pulled from the snow with his lariat. He plowed a path to his cabin, but when a tribe of Pawnee Indians arrived to examine his creation, the buffalo mistook them for hunters and stampeded. The herd dragged that plow all the way to the Missouri River, on the eastern edge of the territory, digging a ditch so deep it filled with water after the snow melted. That ditch is now known as the Platte River.

That was in the winter of 1848, which became known as the Year of the Petrified Snow, because the blizzards were so deep they remained on the ground all summer. This was the same winter that gold was discovered at Sutter's Mill, near Sacramento, setting off the Gold Rush. The snow was an impediment to the gold-crazed men headed west: in fact, it delayed them for a year, so they became '49ers instead of '48ers. After retrieving his enormous plow, Febold ran an ox train carrying would-be miners between Kansas City and San Francisco. On one of his trips to California, he made a detour to Death Valley, where he loaded his wagon with desert sand. The sands of Death Valley have been absorbing the 110-degree sun for thousands of years. After all that time, the heat is baked in. No matter where you take Death Valley sand—to the South Pole, to the Yukon—it remains scorching hot. Febold took it back to Nebraska and sold it to the stranded Gold Rushers for fifty dollars a bushel. They sprinkled it ahead of their wagons, melting the petrified snow and clearing the way to California.

Word of Febold's inventiveness reached the Interior Secretary in Washington, who hired him to redraw the border between Kansas and Nebraska. It's a little-known fact that Kansas and Nebraska were once our most mountainous states, but an infestation of moles had overturned all the mountains, exposing their flat bottoms and erasing the territorial line in the process. Febold plowed a furrow the entire length of the territory, from the Missouri line to the Colorado line. Without a surveyor's training or equipment, Febold couldn't draw a straight line, so his attempted border was crooked, and too far north; it eventually filled up with water and was named the Republican River by President Lincoln. To make up for his lack of surveying experience, Febold found a beehive and poured barrels and barrels of honey into it. The bees inside grew so large that Febold was able to hitch them to a plow, and draw a bee-line between the territories.

In treeless Nebraska, the winds blow freely and fiercely. To amuse himself, Febold built the world's largest kite, which was made from enough fabric to cover one of Nebraska's patchwork counties. The kite was so big it could only be tethered to the Earth with a steel cable. Febold tied it to a cottonwood he had planted on his homestead, but a powerful prairie wind uprooted the tree. Grabbing at the cable, Febold was carried away as well. Just as he began to fear he would never see Nebraska again, Febold had another of his clever ideas. Pulling a slingshot and a handful of birdshot from his pocket, he poked holes in the kite. It began descending toward the prairie, but soon it was falling so fast Febold feared he would make a crash landing. He took off his shirt, and covered half the holes. The kite continued to hurtle earthward, so he took off his pants, too. The kite slowed down enough for Febold to drop into a gully—safely, but stark naked. On his way back to his cabin, Febold had a number of embarrassing encounters with the Pawnee, until one finally took pity on the naked white man and outfitted him with a loincloth. The kite, meanwhile, flew all the way to North Dakota, where it was snagged by a sodbuster whose wife used the fabric to sew garments for all ten of her children, from the swaddling in their cradles to the dresses and morning coats in which they were married.

The winds were not always a source of amusement in Nebraska. Quite often, they gathered themselves into tornadoes. But when the territorial governor learned of Febold's success in ridding his land of mosquitoes, he figured he could do the same to tornadoes. So Febold was hired as Nebraska's first official twister stopper. This was his technique: when he heard a report of an approaching tornado, he jumped on his horse, rode after the twister, lassoed it with his lariat, and tied it up until it ran out of energy and stopped spinning. If the twister tried to escape, Febold chased it into Kansas, where it was no longer his business.

Febold Feboldson was a force of nature, but not even he was stronger than nature itself. He finally met his match against the tornado that destroyed the Bohemian settlement of Cestomihailovich (which is why you've never heard of it). Febold ran the twister down, lassoed it, and took it back home to let it calm down. While Febold slept, the twister busted through the ropes, tore up the Bohemians' cottages, then bound Febold in his own lariat and pushed him down a sand hill. Spinning as fast as a tornado himself, Febold collected so much sand and water he became encased in the mixture, with only his head sticking out. A colony of friendly prairie dogs brought Febold food and water for a week until the Pawnee discovered him and pried him out of his living sarcophagus.

Like most Nebraskans, Febold had rebuilt his cabin numerous times after it was flattened by tornadoes. After the cabin was destroyed for the fourteenth time, Febold built a new one with springs and hinges in every corner. When he saw a tornado coming, he pushed a button and collapsed the entire structure into a flat board. After the tornado was gone, he pushed the button again, and the cabin sprang back into shape. This was such an effective defense against tornadoes it was adopted by every homesteader in the territory, even those who lived in soddies. Pioneers passing through Nebraska were mystified by the sight of entire towns disappearing, then suddenly reappearing again a few hours later. They assumed it was a mirage caused by Prairie Fever, the condition of staring at a flat, monotonous landscape for days on end. Febold's tornado-proofing method is still in use today. The thirty-story headquarters of the Woodmen of the World insurance company, for many years the tallest building in Omaha, was built with springs and hinges, so the entire structure flattens at the push of a button, or so say longtime employees who have ridden out tornadoes there.

There finally came a time when Nebraska became too harsh for even the resourceful Febold Feboldson. That time was the Year of the Endless Drought. We don't know much about the Endless Drought, because there are no records: when the settlers tried to write about it, their ink dried up before it could soak into the paper. Snow flurries turned into dust storms. The drought leached the moisture out of the logs in Febold's cabin, until it shrunk to the size of a doghouse, so he had to crawl through the front door. Febold's cattle grew so thin that he tied sandbags to their tails to prevent them from blowing away. They would have starved to death, if not for another of Febold's brainstorms: he wrote away to an office supply company for a hundred green eyeshades, the kind that telegraph operators wore, and fitted them onto his horses and cows. The eyeshades made the cactus and thistles look like grass, and the herd quickly devoured the spiky plants. Unfortunately, the cactus spikes worked their way out through the animals' skins. When Febold mounted his horse, a cactus needle protruding from the saddle pierced his rump. Needing a new way to get around, Febold captured a pair of hoop snakes, filled them up with whiskey, and put their tails in their mouths. The hooch froze the snakes, so they could function as wheels. Febold attached a seat to the snakes, thus inventing a prairie bicycle he could propel with his feet.

The aftermath of the Year of the Endless Drought was the Great Cactus War. The drought killed off all the foliage in Nebraska except the cactus. After the rains returned, that hardy plant grew to occupy all the empty spaces. When a United States cavalry detachment camped out in a clearing, it was overwhelmed by the swiftly multiplying cacti, which pierced the soldiers to death with their needles. So the army hired Febold to beat back the cactus. After Febold's horses had passed all their cactus needles, and he could ride them again, he released the hoop snakes. One of the snakes didn't want to leave Febold, so he adopted her as a pet, naming her Arabella, after an actress he had taken a fancy to in San Francisco. Arabella's venom was fatal to cacti, so Febold dripped it into a spray gun and killed off the plants so thoroughly they now only grow in the Sand Hills. Arabella donated so much venom for the Great Cactus War she died of exhaustion, and was buried in Arlington National Cemetery with a seven-gun salute.

That was enough for Febold. Having grown attached to Arabella, he cursed the landscape that had caused her death.

"Every wagon train that goes by this cabin is headed to California," he told his grand-nephew, Bergstrom Stromberg. "I'm going there myself. But I'm not going to stay. I'm going to find out why they've got such mild, pleasant weather and so many lush farms, and bring the secret back to Nebraska. Why, if we had seventy-two degree days all year round, and avocado and lettuce farms, our counties would be busting at the seams, just like Los Angeles."

Febold's cousin Hjalmar had died of his broken neck a few years before, so he was finally free to set out for his original destination. If anyone could make palm trees grow on the Great Plains, it was Febold Feboldson. But as far as anyone knew, he never came back to Nebraska. There were rumors he became a bartender in Tijuana, or a trainer whose thoroughbred broke the mile record at Pleasanton Fairgrounds, or the captain of a ship trading for tea in China, or a farmer who grew an avocado as big as an ox's head. There was even a rumor he grew a beard, changed his name to Leland Stanford, and ran for governor of California, although there's not much resemblance between Febold and the politician.

Sadly, after leaving his adopted home state, Febold was forgotten there until the 1920s, when his exploits were rediscovered by a man named Wayne Carroll, a contributor to the *Gothenburg Independent*, a newspaper serving a little prairie town settled by Swedes like Febold himself. Where Mr. Carroll heard the stories we don't know. He may have interviewed Bergstrom Stromberg. But they're certainly more colorful than anything else published in that long-defunct paper. So colorful we're still telling them today.

Peg Leg Joe
and the Songs of the
Underground Railroad

To the slaves of the Southern plantations, the Midwest was a destination on the pathway to freedom. In one of the most famous scenes in *Uncle Tom's Cabin*, Eliza crosses the frozen Ohio River by leaping from ice floe to ice floe, until, "as in a dream, she saw the Ohio side, and a man helping her up the bank." Slaves were not completely free in Ohio, because the slave catchers still operated in the North. But they were able to hide in the series of safe houses known as the Underground Railroad that guided them across the Great Lakes to Canada, where slavery and slave catching were prohibited.

In the case of a one-legged Indiana abolitionist known as Peg Leg Joe, however, the Underground Railroad actually reached into the South. Peg Leg Joe infiltrated plantations in Alabama, providing slaves with a mental map to Illinois by teaching them a song called "Follow the Drinking Gourd," which contained coded references to landmarks on the road north. One spring day in the 1850s, Peg Leg Joe appeared on the plantation where a young couple, Mattie and Henry, had recently "jumped the broom," a slave custom signifying marriage.

Mattie usually didn't pay much attention to the tradesmen who came and went on Mr. Harris's farm. They arrived to shoe the horses, or sweep the chimney, or replace a wagon wheel, and then they were gone, often the same day. None of that was her business, and she had her own work to do, in the kitchen and the laundry.

But in her mind, there was no ignoring the carpenter who came to oversee the building of a horse stable. He was as curious a sight as Mattie had ever seen. In place of the man's right foot, he walked on a wooden peg that pressed a round hole into the dirt wherever he stepped. After the peg-legged carpenter passed by the main house, Mattie and another girl ran outside to look at his footprints. One set was a normal left boot print, the other a disc.

"His name is Joe," reported Mattie's husband Henry, who had been enlisted to work on the stable. "They call him Peg Leg Joe. He used to be a sailor. Used to call at Mobile, which is how he got to know Alabama."

"How did he lose his leg?" Mattie asked.

"He didn't say. Cassius said he heard he lost it fighting with pirates on the Spanish Main, but you know how Cassius makes up stories. Cassius said every time you hear the wind through that big cypress tree, it's Isaac's ghost moaning."

Isaac was a field hand who had died from a whipping administered against that cypress tree, after he'd been caught trying to escape. That had been six years ago. No one had left Mr. Harris's farm since.

That satisfied Mattie's curiosity about the peg-legged man. But apparently, the old sailor continued thinking about Mattie. A week later, after dark, there was a knock on the door of the cabin she shared with Henry. Henry had built it with his own hands after they jumped the broom, so they didn't have to share quarters with the other hands. Henry rolled off their straw mattress and peered through a chink in the door.

"Who's that?" he asked.

"It's Joe," said the voice on the other side of the door.

Henry opened the door. Peg Leg Joe took off his hat and strode into the cabin, imprinting his distinctive tracks on its dirt floor.

"Is there something wrong with the stable?" Henry asked. A late night visit from a white man was always a cause for anxiety.

"No, there's nothing wrong with the stable," said Joe.

"Then why you got to see me in the middle of the night?"

"I had supper with the overseer tonight," Joe said. "He told me I might be missing a pair of hands soon. He said Mr. Harris is planning to sell you to raise money to send his son to college up North, at Harvard."

Henry and Mattie looked at each other. Six months they had been married, after growing up together on this farm. They had courted since they were old enough to be interested in each other that way, and neither had ever been interested in anyone else. If Henry was sold to a distant plantation, they might never see each other again. Mattie could understand why Mr. Harris had singled out Henry: he was only nineteen or so, the tallest, strongest hand on the farm, with years of hard work left in his body before it wore out. Henry might fetch a thousand dollars on the auction block.

"What's any of that to you?" Henry asked, speaking Mattie's mind as well. Why did a man who earned his wages from Mr. Harris care what happened to his boss's slaves?

"I'm not from Alabama," Peg Leg Joe said. "I'm from a place called Whynott, Indiana. And don't ask me why it's called Whynott; we'll be here all night. The first time I ever saw slaves, they were unloading cargo on the docks at Mobile. And then I walked into town—this is when I still had both legs—and saw a man chained up like a criminal, being auctioned off like a breeding bull. Well, I think any man's got the same right to earn his living as I do. Since I lost my leg and quit sailing, I took up carpentry, and I've gone from one plantation to another, plying my trade and helping folks like you escape. I've helped two so far, and neither of them were captured. It's still dangerous, though, so you two think about it. If you're interested, give me a sign while we're working on the stable, Henry, and I'll tell you everything you need to know to make it North."

Peg Leg Joe put his hat back on, tipped it to Mattie, and walked out the door.

"Spring ain't the best time to leave," Henry said to Mattie. "It's better to leave in the fall, when the corn is ripe and you can live off the land."

"You might be sold by then," Mattie said. "And there's something else. I figured it out this week."

"What's that?"

"I'm with child. If we wait, I'll be too heavy. Or we'll have a baby, and we can't travel with a baby."

Mattie and Henry decided right then that they would rather be whipped to death like Isaac than live the rest of their lives apart from each other, as parents of a fatherless boy or girl. The next day, during a break from carrying boards for the stable, Henry nodded at Peg Leg Joe and raised two fingers. Peg Leg Joe nodded back, but he did not return to the cabin that night. Or the next night. Or the night after that. By then, the stable was almost finished, which meant Peg Leg Joe would soon be leaving the farm. Mattie and Henry began to despair of ever speaking with him again. Finally, at midnight on the fourth night, they heard a knock on the door. Peg Leg Joe began by apologizing for his long absence.

"I don't know if anyone saw me the first time I visited," Peg Leg Joe explained. "But if they did, I didn't want them to see me coming here two nights in a row. It might lead to unwelcome rumors."

"The whole place asleep this late," Joe assured him.

"I'm going to teach you a song I taught to the others," said Peg Leg Joe. "It explains the route you'll need to take, and makes it easy to remember."

He began singing:

When the sun comes back
When the first quail calls
Then the time is come
Follow the drinking gourd

The riverbank is a mighty good road
The dead trees show the way
Left foot, right foot, carryin' on
Follow the drinking gourd

The river ends between two hills
Follow the drinking gourd
Another river on the other side
Follows the drinking gourd

Where the little river
Meets the great river
The old man waits to carry you to freedom
Follow the drinking gourd

When he was finished, Peg Leg Joe explained the song's meaning. "When the sun comes back" was a reference to spring, the best time to leave Alabama to ensure you made it to the Ohio River before the winter's freeze. "The river bank is a mighty good road" was the Tombigbee, which could be followed north into Mississippi. Along the way, Joe had carved his distinctive footprints into dead trees, as guideposts to mark the route. The headwaters of the Tombigbee were "between two hills" at the twin-peaked Woodall Mountain. The "river on the other side" was the Tennessee, which flows north into the Ohio. At that confluence, "where the little river meets the great big river," a boat would be waiting to carry them across the Ohio River into Illinois, the southernmost free state. Throughout their journey, as they traveled at night to avoid detection by slave catchers, they should follow the drinking gourd—the constellation known as the Big Dipper, whose handle pointed toward the North Star, a beacon shining over the land of freedom.

"The stable will be finished in a few days, and I'll be moving on," Peg Leg Joe told Mattie and Henry. "I want you to wait at least a week after I leave to run. I don't want word getting around that slaves disappear when Peg Leg Joe is on a plantation. That'll blow my cover, and throwing me in jail will be the nicest thing they'll do to me."

Henry and Joe did not speak again, except when Joe gave an order on the work site. After the job was complete, and Joe rode away, Henry and Mattie waited more than a week to make their escape—until the next full moon, which would illuminate their nighttime travels until they could locate the Tombigbee River. They left just in the nick of time: their absence was discovered when Mr. Harris sent his overseer to their cabin, with orders to chain Henry to a wagon and deliver him to the slave market in Mobile. Furious, the master of the plantation printed up posters offering a $100 reward for the return of his valuable property, and had them nailed up in public squares all over the county.

Mattie and Henry had left the farm with no food and only the clothes on their backs. They feared that carrying bundles would identify them as fugitives, rather than slaves on a master's errand. They followed creeks downstream to the river, listening every night for the cock's crow as a signal to conceal themselves in caves, or the hollows of trees. Even traveling at night was dangerous, because slave patrols rode in the darkness. The penalty for escaping was thirty-nine lashes. Before leaving, the couple had rubbed red onions and spruce pine on their shoes to leave a scent that would confuse the bloodhounds. Sometimes, Mattie and Henry rubbed their backs against trees so the dogs would think they had climbed into the branches. As they headed upstream along the banks of the Tombigbee, they would go entire days without eating, because no fruit or crops had ripened yet. Finally, to feed his wife and the child she was carrying, Henry sneaked onto a farm, seized a chicken that had strayed from its coop at night, and before it could protest, broke its neck with a single twist.

"We're going to have to cook it," Mattie said, when Henry showed her the chicken. "It's too tough to eat raw."

"Someone will smell the fire," Henry protested.

"We can do it in the morning."

"They might smell it then, too."

"If I can't eat, I can't go on," Mattie moaned. "I gotta feed me and this baby. Otherwise I might as well turn myself in while you go north."

To Henry, freedom would have meant nothing if his wife remained in slavery. And the thirty-nine lashes might cause her to lose the baby.

After the night faded into morning, he built a fire in a hollow tree stump, wrapped the chicken in leaves, and placed it inside to roast. The chicken was only beginning to brown when Mattie and Henry heard the barking of dogs. Mattie remembered the words to another song she had heard on the plantation, about running through a creek to wash away a scent, just as Moses and the Israelites had crossed the Red Sea to escape the Egyptians:

Wade in the water
God's gonna trouble the water
Who are those children all dressed in red?
God's gonna trouble the water
Must be the ones that Moses led
God's gonna trouble the water
Wade in the water, wade in the water, children
God's gonna trouble the water

Grabbing the half-cooked chicken, Mattie ran toward a creek they had passed the night before, Henry following behind. The barking was growing louder. They jumped in and sat in the water up to their necks until the barking faded, but they were soon faced with new predators: a pair of water moccasins, writhing on the surface, began circling them. Henry waded to the bank, broke a branch off an overhanging tree, and beat it against the water until the splashing drove away the snakes. When both dangers were gone, they stuffed bits of the sodden chicken into their mouths, choking down the barely-edible meat before hiding themselves for the day.

Mattie and Henry could cook no more meat, and the crops were still too young to eat. The next night, when they stumbled upon a lumber camp, Henry had an idea. The couple concealed themselves in the woods, in a spot where they could observe the comings and goings of the workers. In the morning, an all-black crew arrived with a white overseer, armed and on horseback. After giving his crew their instructions for the day, the white man rode off. When he was confident the overseer would not return until the evening, Henry emerged from the woods and approached the crew. It was risky: there were steep rewards for the capture of escaped slaves, so it was always better not to count on the friendship of strangers. But his wife was hungry, so Henry pressed his luck.

"Sir," Henry addressed the oldest workman, "my wife and I are travelers, and desperately hungry. We were hoping you could spare us some food."

The logger could see that a week's flight had already sharpened Henry's features, pushing his brow and cheekbones against his skin. He gave Henry two strips of beef jerky.

"You go back into the woods where you come from," the logger instructed. "No telling when the boss comes back. I seen the posters for you, and that's as much as he makes in a year. But if you stay where you are, I'll bring some more food tomorrow. I'll leave it in that hollow stump over yonder, so you can come get it after dark."

Henry thanked the man and returned to his hiding place to share the jerky with Mattie. They slept through that day, and then through another day. When the overseer had led away the loggers, and darkness had fallen, Henry looked inside the hollow stump. He found a burlap sack, containing a fugitive's feast: enough jerky and corn meal to feed them for a week. Rationing themselves to two strips a day, and mixing the corn meal with water to make a soft sort of cake (they dared not repeat their mistake with the fire), Mattie and Henry passed the next two landmarks in Peg Leg Joe's song: climbing the pass between the peaks of Woodall Mountain, they found the Tennessee River, and began following its course downstream. Clearly, though, it was going to take more than a week to reach the Ohio, and the boat that would carry them to freedom. Peg Leg Joe had directed them to escape in the spring, so they would arrive before the river froze. That was months. They needed a faster method of travel. Passing a farm one night, Henry spotted a horse tied loosely to a post.

"That would speed us along," he remarked to Mattie.

"You know what they do to horse thieves," she said.

"I know what they do to runaway slaves, too. I'd rather be hung for stealing that horse than whipped and sold off to chop cotton for the rest of my life so young Master Harris can go to college. You wait here."

Henry climbed through the fence and approached the horse, which stared at him silently through spiritless eyes. The horse was a bony, unshorn gelding, but no one would leave a good horse out here in the yard, where anyone could lead it away. The horse looked too old and scrawny to pull a plow. Henry thought he might be doing the farmer a favor by sparing him the trouble of shooting and burying it. His fingers easily untangled the knotted rope, and he led the horse through an unlocked gate.

"Jump on," he ordered Mattie, hoisting her on to the horse's rump. Henry sat on its back, took hold of the bridle, and slapped its neck. The horse cantered forward, along a trail that paralleled the Tennessee. For three nights Mattie and Henry rode that horse, watering it in the river and allowing it to graze in meadows. More than once during that ride, they saw a dead tree on which was carved Peg Leg Joe's footprint, telling them they were on the right course.

On the fourth night, the horse refused to move. Mattie tore a switch off a tree and beat the horse's withers, but it only took a few steps before collapsing to its knees, throwing its passengers into the dirt.

"We done wore it out," Henry said. "We just gonna have to leave it here and move on."

The horse had carried them far. The Tennessee had widened and strengthened, leading Henry and Mattie to believe they were nearing its mouth, where the boat would be waiting. The bag of food was empty, but the growing season had advanced, so they could filch green corn and tomatoes from gardens. Bitter as those vegetables were, they were still nourishing.

Finally, Mattie and Henry climbed to the top of a hill, and saw the Ohio River beneath them. It was the largest body of water either had ever laid eyes on. A moonglade glittered on the surface, as though illuminating the path to freedom. But, of course, they couldn't walk it, and neither knew how to swim. They had to find the boat Peg Leg Joe had told them about. But this being the meeting place of two great rivers, it was also the site of the biggest town either had ever laid eyes on. And they were still in slave territory.

"We just gonna have to go down there late at night, hope nobody sees us, and hope there's a boat there," Mattie said.

Mattie and Henry made their way to the riverfront. Fortunately, a levee shielded them from the view of the townspeople, and no one stirred inside the steamboats tied up along its length. At the point where the little river met the great big river, they saw a rowboat bobbing near the rocky bank. As they drew closer, they could see a white man holding the oars. As they drew closer still, they could see it was Peg Leg Joe. The man who had mysteriously appeared on their plantation and taught them a song that contained the map to freedom had also, mysteriously, beaten them to Ohio River. Splashing through the water up to their knees, they climbed into his boat.

"This is the first night I came down here," Joe said. "You're sooner than I expected."

"We stole a horse," Henry admitted.

"That was good thinking."

As Joe pulled them closer and closer to the Illinois shore, Mattie and Henry both had one thought in mind: as soon as they stepped off this boat, they would be out of the reach of Mr. Harris forever. It wasn't quite so. Once they disembarked, Joe led them to a wagon, instructing them to conceal themselves beneath its load of straw. Then he drove them to a house, where the owner pulled up a rug and opened a trapdoor to a lightless crawlspace. Were they being kidnapped? Was Peg Leg Joe a slave catcher who had posed as abolitionist so he could see them for his own profit?

"This is Mr. Benmark," Joe said, introducing the householder, a bald, bewhiskered man wearing tiny oval spectacles. "He's the first of your conductors on what we call the Underground Railroad. You're not much safer in Illinois than you were in Alabama. At least not in this part of Illinois. President Fillmore signed a law allowing the slave catchers to chase you into the free states, so we're going to get you someplace where his laws don't apply."

From house to house they traveled, sometimes by wagon, sometimes on foot, always in the direction of the North Star, until they arrived in Detroit. There, they hid in the basement of a church run by free blacks who had escaped slavery when the North was still safe for refugees. A steamboat carried them across the Detroit River to a fort owned by the British, who had abolished slavery in all their territories. A thousand miles from Mr. Harris's farm, they were finally free.

Their child was born free, of course. A boy, they named him Joseph. Mattie and Henry settled in Owen Sound, Ontario, the Lake Huron port that was the last stop on the Underground Railroad. Henry found a job on the docks, and Mattie sang in the choir at the British Methodist Episcopal Church. Her favorite hymn was one she had learned back in Alabama, because it expressed the hope that all the congregants had carried with them on their flights to Canada:

Steal away to Jesus
Steal away, steal away home
I ain't got long to stay here

My lord calls me
He calls me by the thunder
The trumpet sound in my soul
I ain't got long to stay here

My lord calls me
He calls me by the lightning
The trumpet sound is in my soul
I ain't got long to stay here

Steal away! Steal away!

Paul Bunyan's Tallest Tales

hot Gunderson was the foreman of a lumber camp in the woods of central Minnesota, outside Brainerd. The old Swede's real name was Torvald, but he was nicknamed Shot because of his skill as a hunter: he had once killed enough deer in one hour to feed a camp of hungry loggers for an entire winter. His hand was no longer as steady as it had once been, but his eyes and his judgment were, and nobody could find better pine in the dwindling North Woods than ol' Shot.

One November evening, after his crew of shanty boys had stacked hundreds and hundreds of logs on the ox-drawn sledges that would be hauled to the narrow headwaters of the Mississippi River, they sat down to a supper of salt pork and beans in the bunkhouse. It was so cold that even the boys sitting closest to the woodstove buttoned their mackinaws to the neck.

"That was one exhausting day," complained a young shanty boy. "I don't think Paul Bunyan himself could have cut down as many trees as we did."

At the mention of Paul Bunyan, Shot perked up.

"You don't think so, eh, Mr. Numminen?" Shot challenged the young man. "Did you ever see Paul Bunyan work?"

"He was before my time," Numminen said. "But everyone knows the stories."

"Everyone thinks they know the stories," said Shot. "But I worked with Paul. Yassir, I did. So Charley Dobey, over here. And Batiste Joe."

Shot motioned at two gray-haired loggers who had been deferentially granted seats near the stove.

"Well, then let's hear 'em," Numminen said. "In fact, I have an idea. Me and all the boys will put up a jug of whiskey for the best Paul Bunyan story among the three of you. Does that sound good, boys?"

The shanty boys nodded eagerly, not because they wanted to hear Paul Bunyan stories, but because they hoped the winner would share his whiskey with the entire camp.

Storytelling was a popular pastime in the logging camps. Books were expensive, and hard to read by kerosene lantern. Also, many shanty boys had never learned their letters, at least not in English. So every logger became a book of his own, passing down the lore of the camps. Every season, the stories grew bigger and wilder, until they had as much relationship to actual history as the legends of Hercules or Samson. The logger telling a tale was given a place of honor on the Deacon's Seat, a split log bench running in front of the bunks. There, Shot Gunderson placed himself and addressed his crew.

"Vell, since I'm the first, I'll start at the beginning, and tell you where Paul came from, and how he met his Babe, his trusty ox," Shot said.

"Paul, he wasn't born in Minnesota, although people here like to claim him. He was born in Maine, near the site of the first lumber mill in this country. He was a big, big baby. It took five storks to deliver him to his parents. When he was a week old, he was wearing his father's clothes. When he was three weeks old, he rolled over and destroyed four square miles of timber. So his parents built him a floating cradle and anchored it off Eastport. Every time Paul rocked, the tides rose seventy-five feet in the Bay of Fundy. After the waves from Paul's cradle wiped out a few fishing villages in New Brunswick and Nova Scotia, the British Navy sailed into the bay and fired its cannons for seven hours until Paul woke up. When he finally did, he stepped out of his cradle and swamped seven warships. So the British seized his cradle and used the wood to build seven more ships. That prevented Nova Scotia from becoming an island, but the tides on the Bay of Fundy still rise and fall more than any place in the world.

"Paul drove a load of logs to the Kennebec River when he was old enough to wear his first woolen trousers. But the Maine woods had been pretty well worked over by the time he grew up. He needed a bigger challenge. He was looking for huge stands of virgin timber that would take a lifetime to cut down, so he came to Minnesota, which was still covered in red pine and Norway pine.

"Paul came here during the Winter of the Blue Snow. The snow was two hundred feet deep, and as blue as the sky. You couldn't tell one from another. Some fellas tried to lay a logging road around a hill that turned out to be a cloud. The snow was so deep that only the tops of the tallest trees poked through. To cut them down, we had to dig holes in the snow, lower the boys down on ropes, then pull the trees out. And oh, you betcha it was cold. It was so cold I slept under forty-two blankets. One morning, I got lost trying to find my way out of bed. By the time they found me three days later, I had just about starved to death. To keep warm, I grew a beard so long I could wrap it around my body and still tuck it into the tops of my boots. When the cook tried to pour coffee, it froze so fast the ice was still hot.

"Anyway, one day Paul put on his snowshoes and went out to fetch firewood. He noticed a pair of ears sticking out of a snowdrift. He yanked on them, and out came Babe. That ox calf was as blue as the snow he'd been trapped in and stayed that way for the rest of his life. Paul bedded Babe down in a barn for the night, but when he returned the next morning, the barn was gone. He found Babe a few hundred yards away, rooting through the snow for a patch of grass, with the barn balanced on his back. He had outgrown it in just one night.

"Babe was so big that when Paul rode him, he had to carry a telescope to see his hindquarters. That ox could pull so much weight that when Paul hitched him to an eighteen-mile-long logging road, with a dozen switchbacks and S-curves, he straightened it out completely, and Paul sold the excess road to Chicago to build Michigan Avenue.

"That ox ate and drank and worked so much that Paul hired a fellow named Brimstone Bill to keep him in food and shoes. Babe ate fifty bales of hay for a snack, and it took six shanty boys to pick the wire from his teeth. Babe got so thirsty hauling logs that Brimstone Bill finally decided to hitch him to a water tank, so he could have a drink whenever he wanted. But as Paul's crew was working its way through Minnesota, the tank sprung a leak up north of Grand Rapids, and the water that flowed out turned into the Mississippi River.

"Whenever Babe lost a shoe, Bill had to open an iron mine so Ole the Blacksmith could forge him a new one. And the shoes were so heavy that when Bill carried one, he'd sink up to his knees in even the rockiest ground. And that, boys, is where Minnesota's Ten Thousand Lakes come from: they're Babe's footprints as he walked across the state."

The shanty boys cheered as Shot stood up from the Deacon's Seat. "Give him the whiskey!" someone cried, but he was shushed by a crowd that wanted more stories.

Charley Dobey took the Deacon's Seat next. Charley had been Paul's right-hand man, left in charge of the camp whenever the great lumberjack went to town. He was a renowned fiddler as well.

"Now I don't need to tell you boys that lumberjacks love to eat," Charley began. The bunkhouse broke into laughter. "We need a big breakfast to get us ready for a big day of chopping, sawing, and hauling logs, and we need an even bigger supper because we're so hungry at the end of it. Well, no team of lumberjacks ever ate more than Paul Bunyan and his boys; not even this one. Paul's cook was named Sourdough Sam, because he made everything out of sourdough except the coffee. He lost a leg and an arm when his sourdough barrel exploded. Paul carved him new limbs out of tree stumps, so he was able to hobble around the kitchen that way.

"The boys loved Sam's flapjacks, but he could never make enough on the bunkhouse stove, so he asked Ole the Blacksmith to build him a bigger griddle. Ole made a griddle so big it was impossible to see across when the steam rose from whatever was cookin'. He hired fifty choreboys to grease it by skating across with slabs of bacon tied to their feet. Then he mixed the batter in drums and poured it out with a crane. Ole also made a dinner horn so heavy only Paul could lift it and blow into it. The first time Paul called the boys in to eat, he blew down ten acres of pine trees. That was a waste of good timber, so the next time, Paul blew the horn straight into the air, which caused a cyclone that lifted up the latrine and carried it into the next county. The boys had to walk all the way there and back every time nature called, until the carpenters could build a new one. After that, Paul sold the horn to the state of Iowa, which used the metal to gild the dome of its capitol building in Des Moines.

"Now, one winter, we were working up northeast of Ely, by the Canadian border. We dumped all our logs onto a frozen lake, figuring we'd float them out in the spring. Well, when the snow and ice melted, it turned out this lake was landlocked. There was no outlet. The nearest stream was ten miles away. But Sam, he had an idea, which, like most of his ideas, involved sourdough. He asked Paul to fill Babe's water tank with sourdough. Paul did, and Babe hauled the tank to the shore, where they dumped all the sourdough in the lake. When the sourdough rose, it flowed over the hill surrounding the lake, carrying the logs with it, all the way to that stream ten miles away. And that's why that particular body of water is known as Sourdough Lake. You can look it up on a map."

Charley Dobey picked up his fiddle. He played it in the bunkhouse every night, to entertain himself and anyone else who cared to listen. Those who didn't care to listen could go stand outside in the snow, because a graybeard who'd logged with Paul Bunyan had earned the right to play his fiddle wherever and whenever he pleased.

"I may not have as many stories as Shot Gunderson," Charley said, "but I can play the fiddle, and I can also sing better than ol' Shot. This is an old ballad about one of Paul's greatest misadventures, the Round River Drive, which happened back in '63 or '64:

At last, a hundred million in,

'Twas time for drivin' to begin

We broke the rollways in a rush,

And started through the rain and slush

To drive that hundred million down

Until we reached some sawmill town.

We didn't know the river's name,

Nor where to someone's mill it came,

But figured this, without a doubt,

To some good town 'twould bring 'em out,

If we observed the usual plan

And drive the way the river ran

Well, after we had driven for

A week or so or maybe more

We came across a pyramid

That looked just like our forty did

Two weeks again; another, too

That looked like our camp came in view

Then Bunyan called us all ashore

And called a council like of war.

Says Paul, "With all this lumbering

Our logs won't bring us a damned thing

And we realized at last

That every camp that we had passed

Was ours. Yes, 'twas then we found
The river was on the round
And though we'd driven many a mile
We'd drive a circle all the while.

"So you see," Charley concluded, "we never did get them logs to a sawmill. They just kept floatin' round and round that river 'til they all rotted away."

Charley Dobey bowed deeply to the shanty boys and yielded the Deacon's Seat to Batiste Joe. Batiste Joe had been born in Quebec, the fourteenth of eighteen children; like many poor French-Canadians, he sought better opportunities in Maine. There, he met Paul Bunyan, and followed him to Minnesota, lured also by tales of taller trees. Joe's black mustache had turned white, and he was now a picturesque little figure in a checked flannel shirt, neckerchief, leather boots, wool socks pulled up to his knees, and a trilby dented in all the wrong places. After so many years in the North Woods, he spoke English as well as French, but his accent left no doubt he was Quebecois.

"This is the story of Paul Bunyan's last big job here in the Nort' Country," Batiste Joe began. "One day, Paul got a letter from the King of Sweden, offerin' him one million dollars to cut down all de trees in Nort' Dakota, so Swedes could farm there. When he was a boy, Paul had been too busy cutting down trees to go to school, so he asked his bookkeeper, Johnny Inkslinger, to read the king's letter to him. Johnny, you know, was such a fast writer that he had a pen connected to an ink barrel by a hose. He wrote back to the king right away, and gave the letter to a stork, who delivered it to Stockholm the very next day.

"Well, that was the biggest job Paul ever had, so he built the biggest camp anyone had ever seen. The bunks was stacked eighteen high: the boys on top used balloons to get to bed at night, and parachutes to get to work in the morning. The dining room was so big that the chore boy who drove the salt-'n'-pepper wagon could only make it to half the tables during dinner, so he spent the night at the other end, and came back the next morning.

"Paul hired the best lumberjacks he could find: the Seven Axemen of the Red River. They was all named Elmer, so Paul could remember to call them, and they each had three axes, and two boys to carry their axes to the river when they got too hot from chopping, so they wouldn't start forest fires. They chopped so fast they didn't have time to come back to the bunkhouse to sharpen their axes, so they done it on stones rolling downhill.

"Those Seven Axemen chopped so fast they chopped down every tree in Nort' Dakota in two weeks. They had double-headed axes, so they swung 'em one way and cut down a dozen trees, then they swung 'em the other way and cut down another dozen. But the problem was, after two weeks, the whole territory was covered in tree stumps. The king was not going to send Swedes to farm on tree stumps. But Johnny Inkslinger had an idea. He knew that Babe didn't like to get his feet wet, so he suggested flooding the entire territory, and having Brimstone Bill put on a pair of hip waders and lead Babe across. Brimstone Bill did that, and Babe stepped from stump to stump, pushing all them stumps deep into the ground. And that's why there's no trees or stumps in Nort' Dakota.

"After he paid the Seven Axemen, Paul took what was left of his million dollars and decided to go to the Pacific Northwest, where the trees is even bigger then in Minnesota. He and Babe ate a big breakfast in

Minneapolis, and were in Seattle for supper. Babe walked right through the Rocky Mountains, sinking up to his knees in rock, and Paul cut down trees as they walked to make a log road for Babe over the stumps.

"Of course, the mayor of Seattle had heard of Paul and Babe. He asked them to dig a harbor for the city, so it could become a great port and attract ships from China. The city hired Andrew Carnegie to build a plow and a scraper so big they used up all the steel made in Pittsburgh in a whole year. But that plow and scraper still weren't big enough to build a harbor, so Paul went up to Alaska and hitched Babe to a glacier. They hauled that glacier down to Seattle, and used it to dig Puget Sound. And that's the last any of us heard of Paul Bunyan."

When Batiste Joe was finished, young Numminen stood up on the Deacon's Seat, with the prize jug of whiskey in his hand.

"First of all," Numminen said, "I need to apologize to Shot, for saying that not even Paul Bunyan could cut down as many trees as we did today. After hearing these stories, I'm convinced Paul could have cut down five times as many trees as we did—and all by himself. Second of all, we have to give away this jug of whiskey. Now who here thought Shot told the best Paul Bunyan story?"

Every shanty boy in the bunkhouse roared at the top of his lungs.

"OK. Now who thinks Charley told the best story?"

The roar for Charley was just as loud.

"And what about Batiste Joe?"

Not even the most sensitive ear could have detected a difference in the volume of cheering for the three old lumberjacks.

"Well, boys, it sounds like a three-way tie to me," Numminen said. "So I'm going to give the whiskey to all three of them to share... and I hope they'll be generous enough to spread some good cheer around the bunkhouse."

It didn't seem possible for the shanty boys to shout any louder than they had for the storytellers, but at that last statement, they did. And so the lumber crew went from enjoying its second-favorite pastime—storytelling—to its favorite pastime of all. The next morning, everyone was an hour late for work, and many of the boys clutched their heads at the sound of falling trees. Shot Gunderson couldn't reprimand them, for he, of course, had drunk more than anyone.

THE HODAG: TERROR OF THE NORTH WOODS

erhaps only Loch Ness, Scotland, is more closely identified with a creature whose existence has never been verified by science than is Rhinelander, Wisconsin. Rhinelander, an old North Woods logging town, was the home of the hodag, a creature whose purported discoverer described it as "a terrible brute who assumes the strength of an ox, the ferocity of a bear, the cunning of a fox and the sagacity of a hindoo snake, and it is truly the most feared animal the lumberman come in contact with." Although more than a century has passed since the last reported hodag sighting in Rhinelander, a fiberglass hodag statue squats outside the Rhinelander Chamber of Commerce, in a pose of imminent attack. Rhinelander High School's sports teams are nicknamed the Hodags. The Hodag Country Festival takes place every summer at a campground outside town. Hodags adorn Rhinelander police cars, while Rhinelanders play softball in Hodag Park, finance

their car purchases at Hodag Auto Loans, and get the oil in those cars changed at Hodag Express Lube.

Some people insist that the hodag never existed, that it was a hoax concocted to lure visitors to Rhinelander's county fair. But to his dying day, the only man to capture and display a hodag would never admit his quarry wasn't real. Eugene Shepard was a timber cruiser, an agent hired to inspect and buy woodland for investors looking to get rich in the logging business. He also speculated in land himself, which had made him one of the wealthiest men in Rhinelander. It did not follow, however, that he was one of the most respected. Shepard was notorious for practical jokes, which usually ended up filling his purse: charging tourists a quarter to smell an exotic "scented moss," which was ordinary moss he had dosed with perfume; devising a mechanical muskellunge to leap out of Lake Ballard, thus convincing summering anglers the place deserved the title "The Greatest Muskellunge Fishing in the World." But it was precisely because of this reputation as a self-promoting mountebank that the publicity-hungry mayor of Rhinelander invited Shepard to a meeting to plan the town's first fair.

"Rhinelander," the mayor told the civic leaders gathered in his office, "is the boomingest town in northern Wisconsin. We're right in the middle of one of the biggest stands of Norway and jack pine in the country. We've got half a dozen sawmills running day and night. We've got paper mills. The Soo Line and the Wisconsin River deliver millions of logs a year. So we need to boost ourselves. Chicago had a World's Fair just three years ago. The least we can do is throw a county fair. I asked you fellows here because I'm looking for an attraction that will draw a crowd. Not just from the county, but from all over the Middle West."

Gideon Marshall, the sawmill owner, suggested a half-mile clay track to race harness horses.

"I doubt we can get Star Pointer up here," he said, mentioning the horse who had just broken the world's record by pacing a mile in under two minutes, "but we can bring in horses from all over the state."

"Green Bay's starting a new semi-pro football team," noted Adolph Gritzmacher, superintendent of one of the paper mills. "We can get them up here to challenge our boys."

Then Eugene Shepard spoke up.

"Any town can put on a horse race or a football game," he declared. "We need an attraction that can only be found in Rhinelander. We need to capture a hodag and put it on display."

The hodag, for those unfamiliar with North Woods lumbering, was a sharp-fanged, sharp-clawed, scaly beast that emerged from the ashes of a cremated work ox. Oxen led hard lives in the lumber camps. They hauled backbreaking loads under the prodding goads of skinners who swore at them in French, or Swedish, or English, or German. Driven to the limits of its strength, a work ox seldom lived longer than six years. Even in a life so brief, it absorbed so much profanity that loggers believed its carcass had to smolder for seven years, to burn away all the curses. At the end of this period, when the pyre finally guttered out, there arose a hodag, a distillation of—and a revenge for—all the cruelty the ox had suffered in its working life.

A primordial saurian in miniature, the hodag was seven feet long and fought the world with sharp horns and a set of spikes running from neck to tail. The hodag was so fierce that it once took an entire party of lumberjacks all day to kill one. Their shotgun shells bounced off its hide, so they attacked their prey with dynamite, setting the hodag on fire. The flaming creature ran through the woods for nine hours, burning down so many trees the lumber camp had to relocate to Minnesota.

"There is no such thing as a hodag," protested Mr. Gritzmacher from the paper mill. "That's just a tall tale you heard from those drunken, lice-infested shanty boys in the camps."

"There is INDEED such a thing as a hodag," retorted Mr. Shepard, who didn't mind being thought of as a charlatan, but hated being called a liar. "I saw one just last week. I was out inspecting a stand of pines north of town, when I smelled something I can only describe as a combination of buzzard meat and skunk perfume. I looked down, and sure enough, there was a hodag. As soon as he saw me, he ran off and hid behind a pine tree. I know where he is, and I can capture him and put him on display for ten cents a peek."

"If you capture a hodag, I'll pay a hundred dollars to see it," Mr. Gritzmacher challenged.

With that pecuniary incentive in mind, Shepard enlisted the aid of the Ancient Order of the Reveeting Society, a group of local sportsmen who fought bears with their fists, out of a sense of fair play. Since a hodag had never been captured alive, the society agreed to the challenge, and helped Shepard dig a pit fifty feet in diameter and thirty feet deep, near the spot where he had seen the hodag. They covered it with poles, hidden under leaves and grass.

"Here's my plan," Shepard explained to the Reveeters. "Now, as you all know, hodags only eat white bulldogs, and only on Sundays. So I'm going to take a white bulldog out to the woods, and when the hodag chases after it, he'll fall right into this pit."

The only white bulldog in Rhinelander belonged to Mrs. Adalbert Weiss, a widow who would never have allowed her sole companion to be used as hodag bait. Fortunately, Mrs. Weiss was a weekly congregant at the Lutheran Church. At noon that Sunday, Shepard lured the dog from its house with an ox steak, attached him to a leash, and spirited him into the woods. There, Shepard walked him around and around the pit. Sure enough, the hodag caught the scent of its favorite prey and came racing through the pines on its short but swift legs. The hodag leaped toward the bulldog and crashed through the poles, into the pit that had been prepared as its prison.

But the hodag's reputation was so fearsome that once it was trapped in its pit, not even the bear fighters of the Reveeting Society had the courage to chain it up and force it into the cage in which it would be displayed at the fair. The hodag ran around and around the margins of its prison, emitting a furious roar of a volume last heard on this continent when the wooly mammoth roamed. A number of Reveeters were overcome by the hodag's breath: black tar coal smoke scented with bulldog carcasses.

The hunting party agreed that only an unconscious hodag could be confined to a cage, and that only chloroform would be potent enough to disable such a vigorous creature. One of the Reveeters, the town's doctor, agreed to fetch a month's supply from his office. While he ran this errand, the hunters laid the logs back over the pit, so the hodag couldn't see his way to freedom. In the darkness, the beast was silent, and remained so until the doctor returned, with a jar of choloform under each arm.

"This'll be enough to knock out a dozen hodags!" he predicted.

But when the logs were rolled away, the hodag was gone. Angrily—

and against the advice of the Reveeters—Shepard clambered down into the pit to find out what had happened to his prize. At the bottom, he discovered a hodag-sized hole. With its long, spiny claws, the hodag had tunneled its way to freedom.

Shepard was not so easily defeated—especially when civic pride and a hundred dollar reward were at stake. He ordered the Reveeters to dig up a tree stump and load it into the wagon he had hired to carry the hodag back to Rhinelander. With the help of Luke Kearney, an artistic friend, he spent the next four months chipping and carving the stump into a life-sized replica of the escaped hodag. When the sculpture was finished, he covered it in an ox's hide and fitted it with bull's horns.

Like his idol, the recently deceased Phineas Taylor Barnum, Shepard was a master at deceiving the public for personal profit. On the day the fair opened, he set up his wooden hodag in a tent illuminated only by the sunlight that leaked through the seams. The sculpture was concealed behind a velvet curtain. Outside the tent, he erected this hand-painted sign: SEE THE HODAG, THE FEARSOME NORTH WOODS LEGEND. CAPTURED AND ON DISPLAY FOR THE FIRST TIME ANYWHERE. 10 CENTS.

When fairgoers paid their dime, they were allowed to peek through the curtain. Unbeknownst to anyone outside the Shepard family, Eugene's sons Layton and Claude had concealed themselves inside the tent. Whenever the curtain parted, they shook the "hodag" via a system of hidden wires, while growling and roaring in an imitation of the cry their father had described for them.

The hodag exhibit earned Shepard hundreds of dollars in admission fees. It was such a hit in Rhinelander he took it to the state fair, in West

Allis. When fair season was over, Shepard set up the hodag in his shed, advertising it at the railroad station as a local attraction. When visitors came within earshot, he called to his sons, "Boys, make sure the hodag is tied up so he doesn't get loose." This was their signal to run to the shed, hide behind hay bales, and shake the hodag.

The one man who wasn't fooled was Adolph Gritzmacher. As a businessman, Mr. Gritzmacher did not part lightly with a hundred dollars. Before he would grant Shepard the reward money, he asked a zoologist from the state university to verify the hodag's authenticity. Fascinated by this possible discovery of a species unique to Wisconsin, the zoologist took a train up from Madison, paid a dime to enter Shepard's shed, and pronounced, "That's just a block of wood." Mr. Gritzmacher never paid Shepard that hundred dollars.

We will never know whether Eugene Shepard actually captured a hodag, or even whether hodags ever existed. They certainly don't today. Andy W. Brown, a friend of Shepard's, invented a steam-driven log hauler which he christened "The Hodag," in honor of the animal whose extinction it would cause. With machines to haul logs, oxen were no longer needed in the lumber camps, and once oxen were no longer burned after short lives of hard toil, hodags ceased to emerge from their ashes.

Shepard was unembarrassed by the discovery of his hoax. For years afterward, he displayed his wooden hodag at his resort on Ballard Lake. He also gathered the Ancient Order of the Reveeting Society for a photo with the "hodag." Whether or not it was real did not matter to Shepard. What was important was that he had fulfilled the task the mayor had assigned him: drawing attention to Rhinelander, which grew so greatly in size and stature that it's now the county seat.

"By no means is all the progress to be credited to the hodag, but the hodag did his bit," Shepard wrote in *New North*, the local newspaper, where he published numerous stories of his hodag encounters. "Not only hundreds, but thousands of people came to view the hodag...and not one of them went away without having learned a little more about north Wisconsin and it is safe to guess that each of those thousands told others what they had seen and heard and in this way the beauties, opportunities and resources of north Wisconsin spread, and many who came out of curiosity only, have come to make their home with us, either permanently or for a few weeks or months of the year. Long live the hodag!"

And indeed, as any casual drive around town today reveals, the hodag is still very much alive to Rhinelanders.

Joe Magarac: Man of Steel

hough Pittsburghers may not see themselves as Midwesterners, their city was once the steel-making capital of the world and thus closely aligned, economically and culturally, with the Middle West. The furnaces of Andrew Carnegie's mills, heated with coal from West Virginia's mines, melted down iron ore from Michigan's Upper Peninsula and Minnesota's Iron Range. Pittsburgh was where the Great Lakes met Appalachia, the two regions combining their riches to produce the world's strongest alloy.

At the time, America's steelmaking heartland stretched eastward to Allentown, and westward to Cleveland, Gary, and Chicago. Like the rest of those cities, Pittsburgh attracted immigrants from Eastern Europe, who didn't speak English, but were willing to work long days in the hot mills. The native-born Americans called the newcomers "Hunkies" — short for Hungarian, even though many came from Poland, Bohemia, Slovakia, Serbia, and Croatia.

Steve Mestrovich came over from Croatia and went to work in a steel mill that smoked and steamed on the banks of the Monongahela River. Along with all the other immigrant steelworkers, Steve lived in Hunkietown, on the flat plain between the hills and the water. His two-story brick house, which was a short walk from the mill gate, had no porch and no front yard. The door opened right onto the sidewalk. When Steve stepped inside every evening, after finishing his shift at the mill, he walked into a house packed with heat from the stove and the smells of his wife's pierogi and *polana kapusta*—lamb and rice wrapped in cabbage.

Steve was the best cinderman in the mill. He swept ashes from underneath the soaking pit, the hot furnace where ingots remained soft until they were ready for rolling. His greatest pride, though, was his seventeen-year-old daughter, Mary. With eyes as blue as the ocean Steve had once sailed across, hair as gold as wheat, and skin fairer than the noblest Old Country ladies, Mary was the most beautiful girl in the Mon Valley. All the young men in the mill talked about her. When Pete Pusic from Homestead ate supper with the Mestroviches after work, his eyes always strayed to Mary, but she was too shy to meet his gaze.

Steve, though, was determined that his daughter should marry the strongest steelworker in the Valley. And so he announced to his besotted co-workers that he was going to hold a contest for her hand: whichever man could lift the heaviest dolly bar would win Mary.

Pete Pusic was already confident that he was the strongest man in the mill, but he began building up his muscles by carrying rails across the shop floor, tucking them under his arms as though they were kindling. By the time of the contest, Pete could hold three in each arm.

On the Sunday of the competition, which was held in a field by the Monongahela, Steve ordered two barrels of Iron City beer from Pittsburgh. His wife brewed prune jack, and cooked enough *polana kapusta* and spice cakes to cover two picnic tables. A truck delivered three dolly bars from the mill: the first weighed 350 pounds; the second 500 pounds; the third weighed more than first two together. It was so heavy that six men had to carry it.

Hunkies gathered from all over the Valley that afternoon. Dozens wanted to compete for Mary's hand, and hundreds more wanted to see who would be strong enough to win her. A gypsy band played Old World waltzes on fiddles and accordions. "*Daj, daj srcek nadaj,*" the gypsies sang. "Give back my heart, and give back a kiss." On a platform draped with bunting sat Mary, wearing a red and green silk dress fringed with lace sewn by her *babcia*. On her hand was a ruby ring Steve had purchased from the company store. A *babushka* covered Mary's golden hair. Steve oversaw the gathering in a necktie, suspenders, and bowler hat, challenging each man who believed himself strong enough for his daughter.

"You been liftin' them rails in the mill," he said to Pete Pusic, "but you think you strong enough to lift the dolly bar? It take six men to carry from truck."

Eli Stanoski from Monessen was the only man in the Valley who could boast he was as strong as Pete. Steve told him to prove it. He gestured to the dolly bars, lying in the grass.

"When I was young man, I lift all three at once," he boasted. "That is how I win Mary's mother."

The men lined up to test themselves against the first dolly bar. It was a hot afternoon, so the straining suitors perspired as though they were standing in front of a three-thousand-degree blast furnace. One dislocated his shoulder pulling on the dolly bar. Another tumbled into the grass when his hands lost their grip. Only three men could lift the first bar: Pete, Eli, and Andy Dembroski, a stranger from Johnstown who had taken the train to Pittsburgh because stories of Mary's beauty had reached his mill. Steve shook his head and grumbled in disapproval: Johnstown mills were puny compared to Mon Valley mills. They only forged a hundred tons of steel a day. How could a Johnstown man be as strong as Pete and Eli?

Pete, Eli, and Andy all lifted the second bar, too, but none could budge the third. Pete seemed to make it quiver, but collapsed before he could lift it from the grass. He looked sadly at Mary, sitting on her throne, and she looked back, crestfallen. Then came Andy Dembroski. Andy stripped off his shirt so the crowd could see the broad chest, barrel arms, and horizon-wide shoulders he had built shoveling ore. He clapped his hands over his head, rubbed them together and gripped the dolly bar. For ten minutes, he heaved and grunted, until the sweat flowed from his blond hair and oozed from his chest. Finally, his hands slipped and he fell flat on his bottom. Andy was picking himself up to try again when the deepest bass voice he had ever heard boomed from the crowd.

"Ho! Ho! Ho!" it chortled.

"Who's laughing at me?" Andy challenged. "You come try this yourself, and when you're done trying, I'll break your neck."

The crowd parted, and out stepped a man seven feet tall, with a back broader than a furnace, and a neck as big around as an ordinary man's waist. He wore a peasant cap atop his head and size 18 work boots on his feet. His pants and his jacket were too small for his enormous frame. With a hand the size of a paddle, he lifted Andy off the ground, then stooped to pick up the dolly bar with his other hand. As the giant waved the squirming steelworker and the unconquerable bar in the air, Steve Mestrovich rushed forward to interrogate this man who was strong enough for Mary.

"Who the heck are you?" he asked the stranger.

"Joe Magarac," the man announced.

All the Hunkies laughed. In Croatian, "magarac" means "jackass."

"Magarac? What kinda name is that for a man?"

"All I do is eat and work like a donkey," Joe Magarac said. He set down Andy and the dolly bar, then took off his jacket and shirt. The crowd gasped to see that his muscles were made of steel, gleaming in the July sun.

"I was born inside an ore mountain," he explained. "I came down to the Valley in an ore train, and now I work in the mill, three shifts a day."

Steve gestured to his daughter. Reluctantly, Mary stepped off her podium. She was still heartsick over Pete's failure to lift the dolly bar, and she certainly didn't want to take the name Magarac. But the Mestroviches were an Old Country family, and a father's word was law.

"You're the strongest man I ever see," Steve said, presenting Mary to Joe. "You're the only man strong enough for my Mary."

Joe Magarac shook his head.

"Mary's the most beautiful girl I've ever seen," he said, "but I have no time for love, only work. I may be made of steel, but I'm not so hard-headed I can't see that Mary belongs with that young man over there."

Joe pointed at Pete Pusic, the second-strongest man that afternoon. It so happened that Father Mahovlic was at the picnic, and he agreed to marry the couple on the spot. The crowd toasted the newlyweds with prune jack, and after the service was over, Joe Magarac had the first dance with the bride, as the gypsy band played a Viennese waltz.

***

After the Mestroviches' contest, the legend of Joe Magarac spread like wildfire all throughout the steelmaking heartland. His foreman posted a sign on the mill fence that read: HOME OF JOE MAGARAC. So widely known was Joe's name that mills in Youngstown, Johnstown, and Gary tried to lure him away. Joe scoffed at their offers. After all, Joe produced more steel by himself than the entire Youngstown mill. Joe's reputation was so great that the best steelworker in Gary visited the Mon Valley to challenge him in a steelmaking contest. After three days, Joe was 3,000 tons ahead. The Gary man gave up and returned to Indiana.

Joe boarded at Mrs. Horvath's house by the mill gate. He ate five meals a day. For breakfast, a dozen flapjacks, a pound of scrapple, an omelet made from two cartons of eggs, a pitcher of orange juice, and two pots of coffee. His dinner, which he carried to work in a washtub, was three whole chickens, a salad made from five heads of lettuce, and a loaf of bread toasted and slathered with lard. During his afternoon break, he ate ten dozen of Mrs. Horvath's pierogis. For supper, three 64-ounce steaks and a half-dozen baked potatoes. And at midnight, an entire pork roast with a bottle of buttermilk. Throughout the day, he washed it all down with a barrel of beer, which he lifted the way other men lift a glass.

Mrs. Horvath tolerated Joe's appetite because he didn't sleep in one of her beds, which left room for another steelworker and his rent money. Joe worked all day and night on the number seven furnace in the open hearth. A living machine, Joe gathered scrap steel, scrap iron, coke, limestone, and melted pig iron to feed the hearth. He stirred the molten steel with his bare hands. While other men tapped the vent hole with a blowtorch, Joe poked it open with his finger. After the steel gushed out, Joe set the ladle himself. Instead of pouring it into molds, he poured it over his hands, squeezing out rails between his fingers.

So prodigious a worker was Joe that he filled the yard with rails faster than the trains could carry them away. There were so many rails piled up by the siding that one Thursday afternoon, the foreman shut down the mill.

"Keep the furnace warm 'til Monday," the foreman told Joe.

When the foreman returned on Monday, he couldn't find his best worker. He walked through the mill, calling out "Joe Magarac!" Finally, a deep voice replied from a ladle. Peering inside, the foreman saw Joe sitting up to his neck in molten steel.

"You're gonna melt in there!" said the foreman, who knew Joe was made of steel.

"I want to melt myself down," Joe said. "There's not enough work in a mill that shuts down on Thursday and doesn't open again until Monday. There's nothing for Joe to do on all those days off. I'm going to melt myself down for steel to build the biggest mill in the world: one that can run twenty-four hours a day, every day except Christmas."

As soon as he said those words, Joe Magarac's head disappeared into the cauldron. When the batch containing his body was tapped and poured into molds, it produced the finest ingots the Mon Valley had ever seen: smooth and straight and strong, with no rough spots or blemishes.

Joe Magarac's name lived on in the mill he helped build. When a man called another man a jackass, it was a compliment, meaning he worked as hard as the strongest steelworker who ever walked through a mill gate. And some say Joe himself lived on. One day, a fifty-ton ladle of steel slipped loose from a crane while three men were standing underneath. Somehow, it hovered in the air long enough for the seemingly doomed steelworkers to escape. When they turned around and saw it crash to the floor, spewing sparks and steel, they also saw, for a moment, a seven-foot man with a back as broad as a furnace door. Then he faded away and was gone.

Joe Magarac may not be as famous to the outside world as Paul Bunyan, but he is still remembered in his hometown, even though the steel mill he sacrificed himself to build has been torn down and replaced with a shopping mall. Outside one of the Mon Valley's few remaining mills, the Edgar Thomson Works in Braddock, stands a statue of Joe Magarac, bending a steel bar, his shirt half open to reveal his gleaming chest. It's a symbol of Pittsburgh's pride in the product it made, and the pride of the hardworking Old Country people who made it.

THE WABASH CANNONBALL

abash Cannonball" is one of the most famous railroad songs ever sung, right up there with "The Ballad of Casey Jones," "Wreck of the Old 97," and "Rock Island Line." Unlike those others, though, it's not about a train that follows a schedule and calls at stations. It's a song from the hobo jungles, as the camps were called, about the last train an old hobo will ever ride.

Does that mean the Wabash Cannonball is not a real train? Well, if you asked a young man who went by the name Lucky Slim when he rode the rails during the Great Depression, he'd tell you he never saw the Wabash Cannonball, never touched it, but it always picked up its passengers.

That second summer of FDR's presidency, Lucky Slim was headed back to Central Illinois. He knew he could get a job walking beans on a farm near Lincoln, and maybe stay on for the harvest after that. Since his own family had lost its farm, in the first years of the Depression, Slim had been a wandering bindlestiff, riding the rails from farm to farm, town to town, trying to earn enough money to feed himself and keep his mother in that rooming house in Springfield. His father was dead. Officially, it had been a heart attack, but really, it was grief over losing a piece of land that had belonged to the family since the state was settled. Slim had just finished a job with the Civilian Conservation Corps, building a lodge at a state park on the Mississippi River. On his way home, he stopped to spend the night at a jungle well concealed in a ravine between the river and the railroad tracks. From there, a hobo could jump a barge or a train, depending on where he was going.

Arriving at dusk, after hopping off a train in Granite City, Slim recognized a couple of faces around the campfire—Missouri Joe and Eighter from Decatur. Hoboes came and went. But after he'd shared in the mulligan stew, contributing a can of beans he'd bought for a nickel, he noticed a familiar shelter. Its walls were bricks and sandbags, its roof an old wooden door, stripped of paint by the elements. Slim peered into the opening and called out "Charlie!"

A face appeared, thinner and paler than Slim remembered from the year before. Pigeon Charlie had earned his nickname because he'd once been so hungry he killed and ate a bird. It may or may not have been a pigeon, but that was the only species everyone around the campfire recognized, and Charlie was a little guy, so it suited him. Now, Charlie looked so withered that his skeleton seemed to be trying to get out through his skin, which was the same ghostly shade as his few remaining hairs.

Slim untied his bindle and offered Charlie the remainder of a Hershey bar, which on this hot night was melted enough for a toothless old man to eat.

"You been travelin', young man," Charlie said.

"I have, old man. What about you?"

"I ain't moved since I seen you here last summer. I'm settin' here waitin' for the Cannonball. I want to make sure it knows where to find me."

"There ain't no train called the Cannonball that comes by here," Lucky Slim said. "That's just an old song they pick around the campfire."

"Son, there had to be train for someone to write a song about," Charlie pointed out. "The Wabash Cannonball won't stop for a kid like you. Only for an old man. It's the last train you'll ever ride. It takes you around to all the towns you've ever visited, then it takes you off the rails forever. I'm gonna see all the old places one more time: not just Rock Island and Peoria, but all the way out to California, where I picked lettuce in oh-four and oh-five, and even down to Mexico, where we had to go for awhile after we got rough with a boss who lifted up our bags on the scale."

Charlie's face wore an eager look that Slim had never seen on that sad old visage. In summers past, Charlie had told his rail stories only after much prodding, and he could not conceal the regret of a man recounting journeys he could never repeat. Now, though, he seemed certain he would hop the trains again.

Charlie offered Slim a spot to bed down under his door. The footsore traveler quickly fell asleep. Some time in the middle of the night, he was awoken by the sound of a horn, and the rumble of an approaching engine. He crawled out of the shelter and climbed the ravine to see which train was passing. The rumble grew louder and louder, until it whizzed past at a keening pitch. He heard the racketing of steel wheels on iron rails, the insistent warnings of the horn. But he never saw a train.

Even before he returned to the shelter, Slim knew Charlie was gone, carried away by the Wabash Cannonball. Out of respect for the old hobo, he sat outside the entrance until dawn. To pass the time, he played "Wabash Cannonball" on the harmonica he carried in his bindle. He sang it for the boys when they buried Charlie by the river. Slim sang the version that appears in *The Hobo's Hornbook*, a collection of railroad folklore from the Depression, adapting them for Charlie. It went like this, more or less:

From the waves of the Atlantic
To the wild Pacific shore
From the coast of California
To ice-bound Labrador

There's a train of doozy layout
That's well known to us all
It's the 'boes accommodation
Called the Wabash Cannonball

Great cities of importance
We reach upon our way
Chicago and St. Louis,
Rock Island so they say

Then Springfield and Decatur
Peoria above all
We reach them by no other
But the Wabash Cannonball

The train she runs to Quincy
Monroe and Mexico
She runs to Kansas City
And she's never running slow

She runs right into Denver
And she makes an awful squall
They all know by that whistle
It's the Wabash Cannonball

There are other cities, pardner,
That you can go to see;
St. Paul and Minneapolis
Ashtabula, Kankakee

The lakes of Minnehaha
Where the laughing waters fall
We reach them by no other
Than the Wabash Cannonball

Now listen to her rumble
Now listen to her roar
As she echoes down the valley
And tears along the shore

Now hear the engine's whistle
And he mighty hoboes' call
As we ride the rods and brakebeams
Of the Wabash Cannonball

Now here's to Pigeon Charlie
May his name forever stand
He'll be honored and respected
By the 'boes throughout the land

And when his days are over
And the curtains round him fall
We'll ship him off to heaven
On the Wabash Cannonball.

RESURRECTION MARY: THE GHOST OF ARCHER AVENUE

ust southwest of Chicago, on Archer Avenue in Justice, Illinois, across the street from Resurrection Cemetery, is a bar called Chet's Musical Lounge. Chet's is a classic roadside tavern, with a pool table, a jukebox, a popcorn machine, and a large clientele of bikers. But Chet's has an unusual tradition: every Sunday, the staff leaves a Bloody Mary at the end of the bar for a ghost. The ghost's name is Resurrection Mary, and she has haunted this stretch of Archer since the 1930s, when she picked up young men dancing to the big bands at the Oh Henry Ballroom.

An old South Sider named Vince was still telling his Resurrection Mary story to paranormal investigators half a century after it happened. When he did, he sounded just as haunted as he'd been the night he met the ghost. Before he went out dancing that evening, Vince put on his favorite suit—a double-breasted gray number with squared-off shoulders—and his most colorful tie, red with Hawaiian hula girls in grass skirts. He cruised Archer Avenue with the top down on his Chevy Cabriolet. The night was warm, and he'd slicked back his hair with enough Brylcreem to keep the wind from mussing it. The Oh Henry Ballroom was going to be jumping, as it always was on Saturdays. Vince had danced to some of the biggest of the big bands there: Harry James, Artie Shaw, Tommy Dorsey. Tonight was just Chet Barsuitis and His Merry Men, from the southwest side of Chicago, but even the local combos knew all the hot numbers on the Hit Parade.

Inside the ballroom, Vince spent the first half hour downing enough Cuba Libres and smoking enough Lucky Strikes to work up the courage to ask a girl for a dance. By the time the band got started on "Jumpin' at the Woodside," he was in a bold state of mind.

Spotting a pretty blonde girl in a white dress, he said, as casually as he could manage, "Hey, it ain't right to stand still for Count Basie. Why don't we cut a rug on this one?"

The girl smiled, and they joined the jitterbugging throng on the parquet floor. The band played a few more fast numbers—"Boogie Woogie" and "Jeepers Creepers"—so Vince didn't get a chance to talk to his partner. That he didn't mind too much. Sometimes girls asked what he did for a living. He was a bookkeeper at the Union Stockyards. Even though he didn't work anywhere near the slaughterhouse, that gave some girls the willies.

When the band segued into "Begin the Beguine," Vince was finally able to get close to his partner. Her name was Mary, and she lived, she said, on Damen Avenue in the Brighton Park neighborhood. That wasn't far from where Vince lived, in the house he shared with his parents (something else he didn't like to tell girls). As they slow danced, he noticed, for the first time, that the girl's hands were cold, her skin brittle. Mary seemed to notice that he noticed it, so he made what he hoped was a light-hearted remark: "Cold hands mean you have a warm heart."

Mary smiled, and they danced together for the rest of the evening. After the final number, Vince offered Mary a ride home; her place was just a straight shot up Archer. But after they had driven north for a few miles, Mary insisted he pull the car over, outside the locked gates of Resurrection Cemetery, the graveyard of Chicago's Polish community. Vince was baffled, but he complied. Mary opened the door, and stepped out onto the roadside.

"I have to go, and you can't follow me," she said.

Then she walked toward the gates, laid a hand on the iron chain that bound them together, and vanished.

Vince spent the rest of the night driving his Chevy up and down Archer Avenue, looking for a blonde girl in a white dress. He drove until dawn, and then, when the cemetery gates opened, he drove through the rows of tombstones, engraved with crosses and angels and names such as Butkowski and Gwiazda and Pietrzyk. He was impelled not simply by the mystery of having seen a ghost, but by the hope that the girl he had danced with was not a ghost, that he could dance with her again on some future night. Catching no sight of Mary, he decided finally to drive to the address she had given him before they got into his car. It was a brick bungalow, on a street of nearly identical houses separated by concrete gangways a few feet wide. Only the adornments on the porches and in the yards—an American flag, a statue of the Virgin in a half-bathtub—differentiated the dwellings.

Vince rang the doorbell. His eyes were red with sleeplessness, his dark beard had not been shaven for a day, and his hair had fallen loose over his forehead. The middle-aged woman who answered the door looked startled by the young caller's dishevelment. She looked even more startled when Vince asked, "Is Mary home?"

"Mary doesn't live here anymore," said the woman, who looked old enough, and enough like Mary, to be her mother. "Mary died in a car accident four years ago. Who are you?"

"I knew Mary in high school," Vince lied; it was the only plausible story for why he had been unaware of her death.

"And you didn't know?"

"I went to college downstate after I graduated," he said. That much was true: he had attended Illinois State University, in Normal. "I just moved back to Chicago."

Looking past the woman, who was still blocking the doorway, Vince spied a framed photo resting atop a piano in the front room. It was the girl he had danced with the night before: an ever-youthful face, never to age. The face of a ghost.

"I am sorry to be the one to tell you," the woman said. "Mary went out dancing with some boys she worked with at Brach's, but they never made it to the dance hall. One of the boys crashed the car into the L at Wacker and Lake. Mary was thrown through the windshield and died on the way to the hospital."

"I'm sorry to hear that," Vince said, retreating down the steps. "I'm sorry for your loss."

"If you want to visit Mary's grave," the woman added, "she's buried in Resurrection Cemetery."

Vince never returned to the Oh Henry Ballroom. Or to Resurrection Cemetery. (He had never learned Mary's last name, so he could not have located her tombstone.) In fact, he was so shaken by having danced with a ghost that he never set foot in a dance hall again. But Resurrection Mary, as the girl's ghost came to be known, continued to haunt Archer

Avenue. When the Big Band era ended, after the war, Mary rested quietly in her grave, because the music she had hoped to dance to on her final night among the living was no longer heard at the Oh Henry. But in the 1970s, her ghost rose again.

Mary's family, not being wealthy, had buried her in a "term grave," a rented plot which only held remains for a quarter century. By the time the term expired, all of Mary's loved ones had joined her in the cemetery, leaving no one alive to renew it. During a renovation, Mary's coffin was removed to an unmarked grave in a remote corner of the cemetery. One night, a suburban police officer received a report of a woman in a white dress walking through the grounds of Resurrection Cemetery. When he arrived at the gates, he found two bars pried apart, with scorch marks where a pair of hands would have gripped them. The following year, a couple driving down Archer Avenue saw a girl, wearing the same white dress, lying in the street. The man at the wheel swerved to avoid her, but she disappeared before his tires could make contact. In the 1990s, the owner of Chet's Musical Lounge was pulling out of the driveway when he saw a man running up the road, waving desperately.

"I need to use your phone," the man said, in a stricken voice. "I hit a woman back there, but I can't find her body."

"Was she a blonde woman in a white dress?" the owner asked.

"How did you know?"

"That was Resurrection Mary. Don't worry, you didn't hit anyone; you saw a ghost."

Despite these reappearances on Archer Avenue, Mary has yet to drink her Bloody Mary at Chet's. When a ghost is roaming your neighborhood, though, you have to be ready to soothe her restless spirit.

ROSIE THE RIVETER: THE WOMAN WHO BUILT THE B-24

he most famous poster from World War II does not depict a soldier; it depicts a woman. She wears a red polka-dotted kerchief over her hair, and she's pulling up the sleeve of her blue work shirt to reveal a powerful bicep.

"We Can Do It!" the legend beneath the picture declares.

The woman in the poster is Rosie the Riveter, who was meant to represent the millions of American women who worked in munitions factories while their fathers, brothers, husbands, and boyfriends fought overseas. The war changed life for American women, who learned that they could do jobs that had previously been considered "man's work." It also changed lives for rural families, who left their farms and followed the "Hillbilly Highway" up north to the factories of Michigan, which switched from building cars to building tanks and airplanes.

There was more than one riveter named Rosie working in the war industries, of course. This is the story of a Rosie whose journey took her from a backwoods farm in Kentucky to a bomber plant in Michigan. When the Japanese bombed Pearl Harbor, Rosemary McCumber didn't hear about it on the radio. The electrical lines had not yet reached the farm in Kentucky where she and her husband Hill supported themselves and their two children, Billy and Doris, on a stingy crop of beans and corn, eggs from the chicken coop, and a hog every Christmas. As the McCumbers were unhitching their horse after a long service at the Cumberland Presbyterian Church, a neighbor boy came running up the dirt road. He had just been in town, where he'd heard the news.

"Japs attacked us," he said, out of breath. "I'm goin' to Lexington to join the Navy."

"You ain't but fifteen," Rosemary said. "They won't take you."

"I'm almost six feet tall," the boy said. "I'll tell 'em I'm eighteen. I was born at home, so I ain't got a birth certificate."

Hill saddled up the horse and rode into town to gather more news. When he returned, he told Rosemary that he, too, planned to enlist in the armed forces.

"You can get a deferment," Rosemary argued. "You're a farmer, and you got two kids."

Hill grimaced.

"My dad was in the first big war," he said. "My great-grandad and his brothers were in the Civil War, on both sides. Their dad was at Vera Cruz with General Scott. I ain't gonna be the first McCumber who isn't there when his country needs him. What am I gonna tell Billy when he asks what his dad did when the Japs attacked us? Anyway, this farm barely feeds us, much less an army. My combat pay will go a long way here."

And so, that spring, Hill McCumber became a private in the United States Army, while Rosemary was left alone on the farm to plant the crop. Mama had been living with them since Papa died, so she could cook and look after the children, but Rosemary had to rise at five every morning to gather and candle the eggs, milk the cow, feed the hog and hitch up the horse for plowing. In the evenings, after the children went to bed, she had always enjoyed reading by the kerosene lantern—short stories in *Collier's*, spiritually themed novels she traded with other women in the church sodality—but now she was so exhausted at the end of the day she didn't have the energy to light the lamp, much less concentrate on a line of print. With the help of Hill's army paychecks, Rosemary fed the family through the fall, while canning enough fruits and vegetables and smoking enough meat to survive the winter, but she dreaded another planting season. America had been in the war for less than a year, but with Hitler occupying half of Russia and the Japs taking over the Philippines, we were going to be in this one for a long, long time.

That October, Rosemary received a letter from her cousin Alma. It bore an exotic, unpronounceable postmark: "Ypsilanti." Preoccupied as she was with the harvest, Rosemary laid the letter aside for several days. When she finally opened it, this was what she read:

Dear Rosie,

I know you've been busy with the farm, so you might not have noticed I left town. I got a job here at Mr. Ford's plant in Michigan, building engines for bombers! I went into Lexington to see a movie with Clay Gilmore, and I saw a poster that said "Women in the War, We Can't Win Without You," with a photo of a gal holding a rivet gun. Well, I asked around, and I found out they're hiring gals to work in the factories while the boys are overseas. So I got on a bus and came up here and they hired me right away. They like the gals because our hands are better at handling the little engine parts, and they're paying me a dollar an hour.

Let me know if you hear anything about Clay. He's not answering my letters. He thinks I left on account he's 4-F because of the rheumatic fever he had when he was little. If you see him, tell him I just had to get away from the farm. I'm sharing a room with three other gals, but they're building houses for families, and there's a nursery if you want to come up here with Billy and Doris.

Love,

Alma

A dollar an hour? That was as much as the farm paid in a whole day. Leaving the children with Mama, Rosemary paid a dear price for a bus ticket from Lexington to Ypsilanti, where she looked up Alma at the address on the envelope. Two days after her arrival, with the help of Alma's recommendation, Rosemary was accepted for training as a riveter on the bomber assembly line. Rosemary had never held a "public job," which required working indoors and punching a time clock. When she walked into the Willow Run plant for the first time, and saw the shooting sparks, and heard the thump of rivet guns, and saw the thousands of coveralled men and women clambering around bomber bodies as big as whales, she thought she must be in the biggest, loudest room in the world. This was not simply a country girl's culture shock. Willow Run was three-and-a-half-million square feet, the largest factory every built. Inside were 40,000 workers—a quarter of them women. They were producing one B-24 Liberator, an airplane with over a million parts, *every hour.* There was no way the Japs and the Nazis could shoot them down that fast. Rosemary was just as proud of the McCumber family's military tradition as Hill. This would be her way of carrying it on.

With her first paycheck, Rosemary sent for Mama and the children. They all moved into a village of prefabricated houses near the plant. It was the first time any of them had lived in a home with electricity or running water. On her first day off, Rosemary took the children downtown to buy their first winter coats and their first pairs of store-bought shoes; Billy and Doris walked stiffly for a week, until the shoes were broken in. She wrote to the neighbor who was looking after their farm, offering to sell him the livestock and rent him the land. He sent back his acceptance, along with a money order. Then she wrote to Hill, who was now in England, telling him she had left the farm to work in a munitions plant.

"Darling, that's the best thing you could have done for me and for the USA," Hill wrote back. "We already got a flock of B-24s here, and from now on, every time I see one, I'm gonna think of you again. The farm will have to be put on hold until this war is won."

Once her training was finished, Rosemary went to work fastening the aluminum skin to the center wing section of the bombers. Hour after hour, she pounded rivets into the plane's ribbing. Every B-24 was held together with 700,000 rivets; by the end of each shift, Rosemary's aching arm felt it had pounded in at least half that many.

Every noontime, during the day shift lunch break, Rosemary took off her hard hat, so only a handkerchief held down her sweaty red hair. She rolled up the sleeves of her blue coveralls and took a ham sandwich out of a lunchbox on which she had painted "ROSIE" in white letters. A photographer from the Office of War Information was visiting Willow Run one day to take pictures for a poster recruiting women to join the war effort. He spotted Rosemary stretching and flexing her arm, to get the stiffness out.

"Ma'am, can you hold that pose for a moment?" the photographer requested.

"What for?" Rosemary asked.

"A recruiting poster, to encourage more women to work in the factories."

Well, she'd gotten this job because her cousin Alma had seen a recruiting poster, so she could take a break from lunch to help bring more women into the plant. The photographer snapped off a few frames, and moved on down the assembly line. Rosemary forgot all about the picture until Lois, one of the other gals at the plant, showed her a magazine cover painted by America's most popular illustrator: it depicted a brawny-armed red-haired woman sitting with a rivet gun on her lap, holding aloft a sandwich. Her lunchbox was labeled "ROSIE."

"Rosie, that looks just like you," Lois insisted.

"Oh, that could be any gal in the plant," Rosemary said. "I'm not the only riveter named Rosie. It's probably some gal building a ship in California."

But the gal on the magazine cover was striking the same pose Rosemary had struck for the photographer, flexing the arms she had built up on the farm. She hadn't been holding a rivet gun on her lap, but the illustrator had to show what kind of work she was doing; if he had actually painted her riveting, the readers would not have been able to tell she was a woman. When workers put on coveralls, hard hats, and goggles, distinctions of sex disappeared. Walking down the line, you couldn't tell whether a man or a woman was riveting, or welding, or spraying paint. The tools and the uniform made everyone anonymous, and equal.

Despite Rosemary's dollar-an-hour paycheck, the family's only indulgence was a radio, to keep up with the war news, since Hill was now fighting in the deserts of North Africa. On Saturday nights, Doris and

Mama loved listening to *Your Hit Parade*, on a Detroit radio station. Every week now, the program featured a young woman singing about "Rosie the Riveter":

"Rosie's got a boyfriend, Charlie
Charlie, he's a Marine
Rosie is protecting Charlie
Workin' overtime on the riveting machine"

"Mama, that's you!" Doris exclaimed, when she first heard the song. "Your name is Rosie, and you work on the riveting machine!"

"That is not me," Rosemary corrected. "I do not have a boyfriend named Charlie, who's a Marine. I have your father, who's in the Army. But I am going to buy a war bond for you and your brother. Twenty-five dollars apiece, and I'll buy you each a horse when they mature, because you'll be old enough by then."

Lois suggested that Rosemary sue the illustrator and the "Rosie the Riveter" songwriters, for appropriating her name and her image.

"They're selling millions of copies of the magazine and the song," Lois said. "You could get enough money to quit this dirty plant."

"I don't want to quit the plant," Rosemary said. "If that picture and that song help the war effort, that's good enough for me."

When a Hollywood actor came to Willow Run to make a short film promoting war bonds, he heard there was a riveter named Rosie working in the plant and insisted on including footage of Rosemary pounding rivets in a B-24. It was for the war effort, so once again Rosemary posed for the cameras.

When the war ended, the Willow Run plant shut down. The army didn't need any more bombers. The men went to work in Mr. Ford's other plants, building new cars for drivers who had been nursing along their old jalopies since Pearl Harbor Day. The women were given pink slips and told to go back home to their families. Eighteen million women had built weapons during the war, but it was understood they had been doing men's jobs, and that there would be no place for them in the factories once the soldiers came home.

Hill, who was part of the force occupying Germany, was not discharged from the army until a year after V-E Day. In the meantime, Rosemary took a job as a cook in a dormitory at the university in Ann Arbor, and she moved the family into a rooming house near campus. They were living there when Hill returned.

"We can all go home to Kentucky now," he said.

But Rosemary had other ideas. After four years in this modern, urban world, she didn't want to go back to that primitive farm, where they worked as laboriously as pioneers just to survive. For the entire time Hill was in Europe, Rosemary had supported a family, paid bills, and learned to deal with bosses, union stewards, doctors, and schoolteachers. Now, Hill was asking her to return to a life of rural isolation, in which her only social contacts were at church on Sundays. Rosemary knew Kentucky had changed. The war had brought electricity, plumbing, and paved roads to their county. But that also meant that Kentucky would have no place for a yeoman farmer: agriculture was becoming a business rather than a way of life.

The war had changed Rosemary, too.

"You can make more money here than we ever dreamed of back home," she told Hill. "I'm sure you can get a job at Ford's. You fixed tanks and jeeps during the war. You're a veteran, and everyone's gonna want a new car now after making their old ones last through the war. We can buy the kids new shoes and new clothes every year, and we can even send them to college if they want."

"That farm's been in my family over a hundred years," Hill said.

"We don't have to sell it. We can keep renting it out. We can even build a bigger house there."

Hill agreed to stay in Michigan for a year. He got a job on the assembly line at Ford's in Dearborn. That meant Rosemary had to quit her job at the cafeteria, but she never stopped working, since both Billy and Doris were in school now. Using the homemaking skills she had learned on the farm, she took in alterations as a seamstress. She also drove a school bus. Hill impressed his foremen at Ford's with his ability to repair machinery, and after a year, he was invited to join an apprenticeship program for tool and die makers. The McCumbers prospered so much that Rosemary could afford to open a beauty shop. Back home, she had always fixed her sisters' and cousins' hair, because none of them could afford to go into town. She called the shop Rosie's and didn't mind when people called her Rosie the Riveter, because it was good for business. She put up a print of the magazine poster, and another poster of the woman in the red bandana. A local newspaper published a story headlined "REAL LIFE 'ROSIE THE RIVETER' OPENS SALON," and some of the gals from Willow Run stopped in to get their hair done.

After the children graduated from high school, Billy went to work at Ford's, like his father, while Doris went to the teacher's college in Ypsilanti and a got a job at an elementary school in Dearborn. Hill retired from Ford's after putting in his thirty years, and took Rosie back to Kentucky, to the big house they had built on the McCumber farm with his factory paychecks.

"I thought I was marrying the prettiest girl I'd ever met," Hill told her when they moved back home. "But I married the smartest and hardest working, too. We'd have lost this farm if we'd come back down here and tried to work it again. That old war ended being good for something, I guess."

LE GRIFFON: *The Ghost Ship of the Great Lakes*

he French largely disappeared from Middle West after losing it to the British during the French and Indian War. They left behind only a constellation of nascent cities, whose names their English-speaking conquerors have persisted in mispronouncing: Detroit, St. Louis, Versailles, Des Plaines. Yet the French haunt the Middle West still. Not only Nain Rouge, who has yet to be exorcised from Detroit, but La-Salle, who built the first ship ever to sail on the Great Lakes. *Le Griffon*, as he christened it, disappeared on its maiden voyage, and still appears to rookie sailors to remind them of the hazards of their new career.

Every sailor knows that autumn is the deadliest season on the Great Lakes. As winter tries to force its way down from Canada, it collides with lingering warm air, generating violent storms that "have drowned many a midnight ship with all its shrieking crew," in the words of that famous maritime chronicler Herman Melville.

Don Pryzbyla had a run-in with *Le Griffon* during his first year on the boats. He had graduated high school in Calcite, as sailors call the limestone port of Rogers City, and gone to work on the *Ernest F. Hobby*, which carried the chalky white rock to the mills in Gary and Chicago, where it was mixed with iron and coke to make steel. Sailing was dangerous—just two years before, another Calcite boat, the *Carl D. Bradley*, had carried 33 sailors to the bottom of Lake Michigan. But it paid better than the quarry, and sailors got the winters off.

All that summer, the *Hobby* had sailed on placid waters. But as the boat made an October run up Lake Michigan, after dropping off a load of limestone at U.S. Steel South Works in Chicago, a squall arose. The *Hobby* wallowed over heaping waves, which splashed across the deck, driven by forty mile per hour winds. Deckhands sheltered in their berths, peering out at the storm through portholes obscured by rain. As third mate, Don was in the pilot house, standing the midnight-to-four watch, when the captain of the ship—who all the crewmembers referred to as the Old Man—ordered the boat to seek anchorage inside the breakwater at Milwaukee. As the *Hobby* headed for its safe harbor, Don spotted another ship. It appeared to be headed in the same direction. He was perplexed, because this vessel was no more than a hundred feet from the *Hobby*—close enough for a collision—but had not shown up on the radar. Don was also perplexed because this was not a modern steel laker, but an ancient wooden boat, with sails torn to shreds by centuries of storms, and a carved prow washed colorless by wind and water.

Don walked to the window and alerted the wheelsman.

"We got another ship right to starboard," he cried in a panicked voice.

The wheelsman gazed out the window. He saw nothing but rain.

"Is it an old schooner, with tattered sails?" he asked Don.

"Yeah, that's it."

"That ain't no ship," said the wheelsman, who had been piloting boats

boats since before the war. "That's a ghost. It's the *Griffin*. The first ship that ever sailed on this lake, and the first that ever sank here. I saw it during my first storm, too. Ask the Old Man about it when we get to Milwaukee. He loves to tell that story."

The Old Man, the master of the *Hobby*, was proper and pedantic. He always wore his billed master's cap and his brass-buttoned jacket, with a gold stripe for every half-decade on the Lakes. Wherever he walked on the boat, an anxious cone of silence descended over his crew. Even so, he only spoke to the mates and the chief engineer. But when he heard Don had seen the *Griffon*, he invited the young sailor into his office. Its shelves were filled not only with the nautical manuals he followed so scrupulously, but with volumes of maritime history. Had the Old Man not become a ship's captain, he might have been a high-school teacher, or a minister. He asked Don to sit down, and told him the story of the *Griffon*, as though it were a lecture he had delivered to generations of students.

The Old Man began by telling Don about Rene Robert Cavalier, the greatest explorer who ever set foot on the North American continent. He was the first European to descend the Upper Mississippi, and he hoped to discover a route from that great river to the Gulf of Mexico, which he believed would link France to the trading ports of China and India. But his explorations had left him deeply in debt to the moneylenders of Montreal. If they were to continue, he needed a source of income. So Cavalier (who was better known by his title, the Sieur de la Salle —or simply La Salle) decided to enter the fur trade. He dispatched a crew of voyageurs to the Illinois Country to barter with the Indians on his behalf. And then he set out to build a ship, which would collect his pur-

purchases and carry them back to Montreal, where he would sell the furs and settle all his debts. La Salle also knew that a great ship on the Upper Lakes would allow him to control the Northwestern fur trade.

According to the Old Man, La Salle laid the keel in the winter of 1679, on Cayuga Creek, which flows into Lake Erie, just west of Niagara Falls. It immediately drew suspicion from the Seneca. They had never seen such a large vessel. They called it a "floating fort," or a "big canoe." A Seneca warrior tried to kill the blacksmith who was forging the ship's cannons, but the blacksmith fended him off with a hot poker. Another group of Indians plotted to burn the ship down, but their destructive designs were thwarted by a tip from a squaw friendly to the French. Luckily for La Salle, most of the Seneca were off hunting while he was building his ship, but a Seneca prophet named Metiomek scolded him for introducing such a monstrosity to the Iroquois Country. In a booming voice, the Old Man quoted what Metiomek told the chief:

"Great Chief, you are too proud. You have shown contempt for the Great Spirit who rules all things, and you have set up an evil spirit on His throne. Beware, darkness like a cloud is ready to envelop you. A curse rests on you and your great canoe. She will sink beneath the great water and your blood shall stain the hand of those in whom you trusted!"

The old man then continued his tale. When the ship was finished, she was forty feet long, eighteen feet wide, and weighed sixty tons. A single mast lifted her sails to catch the winds, and five cannons protruded from each side of her hull. La Salle named her *Le Griffon*, after the mythical beast with the head of an eagle and the body of a lion. He did that because the griffin was on the coat of arms of Count Frontenac, governor of New France. A man deeply in debt always wants to get in the good graces of a rich nobleman. A woodcarver shaped the prow in the beast's image, and La Salle bragged that "the griffin will fly above the crows," by which he meant that Frontenac would overcome the black-robed Jesuits' influence among the Northwestern Indians.

Le Griffon was launched on the seventh of August, sent off with a three-cannon salute, a Mass, and a singing of "Te Deum," a Gregorian chant for God's mercy. Besides La Salle, some of the passengers were his faithful sidekick, Henri de Tonty; Father Louis Hennepin, a great explorer in his own right; and Luke the Dane, a giant wheelsman who piloted *Le Griffon* out of Cayuga Creek and onto Lake Erie. On its first day out, *Le Griffon* passed Long Point, on the north shore of the lake; on the second, it passed Point Pelee; on the third, it sailed up Wa-we-a-tu-nong, which was the Indian name for the river where Cadillac would found his great city a few decades later. The voyageurs on board stepped out and killed deer for the ship's larder and plucked grapes for wine.

"This Father Hennepin could see Detroit was going to be a big deal," said the Old Man.

He took down a copy of Francis Parkman's *La Salle and the Discovery of the Great West* from his shelf, and from a bookmarked page, read Hennepin's description of the future site of Detroit:

> We found the country on both sides of this beautiful strait, adorned with fine open plains. Any number of stags, deer, bear (by no means fierce, and very good to eat), *pouler d'indes* (wild turkey) in abundance, and all kinds of game. The vessel's guys were loaded and decked with wild animals our French and Indian hunters had shot and dressed. The islands on both shores of the straits are

covered with primeval forests, fruit trees, like walnuts, chestnuts, plum and apple trees, wild vines loaded with grapes, of which latter some were gathered, and a quantity of wine was made. The vast herds of deer surprised us all, and it appears to be the place of all other where the deer love to congregate.

The day after it left Detroit, *Le Griffon* sailed into a little lake. This was August eleventh, the feast day of Sainte Claire of Assisi, a follower of St. Francis, so La Salle named his new discovery after her, although when the Americans took over, they changed the name to Lake St. Clair.

When *Le Griffon* got out onto Lake Huron, a terrific storm blew in. Hennepin and all the Frenchmen prayed to St. Anthony of Padua, the patron saint of lost things. Luke the Dane, who wasn't a Frenchman, or even Catholic, cursed at La Salle from bringing him to die on French waters. At Michilimackinac, *Le Griffon* fired its cannons, and was surrounded by the bark canoes of a hundred Odawa who wanted to get a closer look at the floating fort. They were like minnows inspecting a shark.

Finally, *Le Griffon* put in at Green Bay, where La Salle's voyageurs had collected twelve thousand pounds of furs, worth sixty thousand francs—more than enough money to pay off his debts. The voyageurs loaded the furs onto *Le Griffon*, and La Salle ordered Luke the Dane to sell them in Niagara, then meet him back at the mouth of the St. Joseph River, in Michigan, where he planned to build a fort. It was mid-September by then. As La Salle, Hennepin, and the rest of their party paddled down the shore of Lake Michigan, they constantly had to beach their canoes to escape foul weather.

Le Griffon was never heard from again. Some people say it sank in an autumn storm. If that's true, it would not only have been the first ship on the Great Lakes, but the first shipwreck. Others say the ship was captured by Indians, who had always seen *Le Griffon* as a vehicle for the French to intrude on their territory, and burned to the waterline.

"La Salle was like a lot of big shots then and now," the Old Man told Don. "He was obsessed with his men's loyalty."

La Salle thought his men had sunk the boat themselves and made off with his furs and hides. He even wrote a letter to the authorities in Quebec, claiming an Indian boy had told him that a tall white man, about the size of Luke the Dane, had been captured and brought to his village as a prisoner, carrying a bundle of furs he intended to sell to the Sioux. Whatever had happened to *Le Griffon*, La Salle was in a bind. He couldn't pay his creditors, so they seized his property in Montreal. *Le Griffon* had also contained the rigging for a ship he had planned to build at Fort Crevecoeur, a fort he established that winter on the Illinois River, where Peoria is today, so he could sail down the Mississippi. So La Salle walked all the way from Illinois to Montreal, begged another loan from Count Frontenac, and brought a whole new batch of supplies back to Fort Crevecoeur. And with those supplies, he built another ship, and sailed down the Mississippi to the Gulf of Mexico.

"Now, I said *Le Griffon* was never seen again," the old man said to Don, "but you know that's not true, because you saw it yourself. It's been reappearing on the Lakes ever since it disappeared from this corporeal world. All the way back in '01, the year I was born, a ship headed from Chicago to Muskegon saw it pass right in front of her bow, all covered in ice, just as the sky was darkening for a storm. I saw it during my own first year on the Lakes. I was standing watch during a storm, when I saw that ragged ship headed straight for our hull. I rang the alarm bell to warn the wheelsman, but just as the ship was about to collide with us, she disappeared. When I told the older sailors what I'd seen, they all said it was "the *Griffin*"—they used the English name. I took that as a warning. The first ship ever on Lake Michigan, and it sank in a September storm!

"I'm a hawsepipe. I worked my way up from where you are to where I am today." The old man touched the bill of his cap with two fingers. "I've always been a captain who guarded the lives of my men. I've never pushed through a storm just to get a tonnage bonus, like some guys who've ended up at the bottom of the lake. If you decide to stick with this and work your way up, I'm sure you'll do the same, because you saw *Le Griffon*."

Don did work his way up, to become the master of his own boat, the *Joseph A. Block*. During his first season, he heard that a rookie deckhand had reported seeing a rotting wooden ship float out of the morning fog. The ship, he insisted, had disappeared just before it collided with the bow. Don took the kid into his office, and told him the story of *Le Griffon*, just as the Old Man had told it to him.

BESSIE: THE LAKE ERIE MONSTER

f you live in Northeast Ohio, you've probably heard of Bessie, the Lake Erie Monster. You may have drunk an IPA called Lake Erie Monster, which is produced by the Great Lakes Brewing Co. of Cleveland. Or you may have watched the Lake Erie Monsters, a minor league hockey team that plays in Quicken Loans Arena. But have you ever seen the Lake Erie Monster in real life?

Two fishermen, who liked to spend summer Saturdays out on the lake with a pole in one hand and a can of Schlitz in the other, saw Bessie one terrifying afternoon in the 1980s. Frank and Joe left the East 55th Street marina in Cleveland just after dawn, in Frank's twenty-foot fishing boat, the *Cool Breeze*. They had a cooler full of beer and sandwiches and a carton of worms they'd purchased from Vic, the old Croat who ran the bait shop. Lake Erie was waveless, windless, and as smooth as a blue tarpaulin stretched from Detroit to Buffalo. Frank and Joe motored fifteen miles from shore, set their lines, pulled the brims of their caps over their eyes to shade them from the white sun, and cracked open a couple of tall boys. By the afternoon, the six-pack was gone, replaced in the cooler with the glittering corpses of walleye and perch. They planned on picking up another six-pack on the drive back to Joe's place, where they'd gut and fry the fish to eat with greens and cobbler. Mrs. Joe Deshazer made the best peach cobbler in East Cleveland.

The two anglers were hauling in their lines when the water beneath them began to heave and swell. Frank grabbed the side of the boat. His foot reached forward in awkward half step, as he struggled to keep his balance. Frank and Joe looked each other bewildered. Storms whip up quickly on Lake Erie, the smallest and shallowest of the Great Lakes, but it had been as gentle as a pond all day, and still no waves disturbed its glossy sheen, no storm clouds darkened the Canadian shore. Frank was pitched against the railing. He looked down into the lake and saw a black shape, longer than his boat, gliding beneath the surface. The wavering water blurred the creature's shape, but Frank thought it looked like the biggest alligator he had ever seen.

It was no alligator. The creature gripped the hull of the *Cool Breeze* with its long arms and began rocking the boat back and forth. The cooler slid across the deck, struck the railing, and tumbled into the water, its lid flying off and releasing the day's catch back into the lake. Shaking and tingling, fear filling his body like helium, Frank stumbled to the captain's chair and fired up the engine. As he opened the throttle, the creature released its grip, and the *Cool Breeze* sped back to Cleveland at top gear. As soon as he calmed down enough to let go of the wheel, Frank radioed the Coast Guard.

"I just saw a creature that looked like a really long alligator," he reported. "The damn thing grabbed my boat and tried to tip it over! I was shaking like a bell!"

"Sir, can you tell us what color it was, how long it was?" the officer on duty asked.

"It was black, like the Creature from the Black Lagoon, and it was longer than my boat, and my boat is twenty feet long."

"Sir, it sounds as though you saw the Lake Erie Monster. If you give us your coordinates, we'll send a cutter."

The Lake Erie Monster was Cleveland's creation. During the city's industrial heyday, the Cuyahoga River—the slow, sinuous channel that carried the effluent of steel mills, paint manufacturers, and chemical plants into Lake Erie—was one of the filthiest bodies of water in the world. The Cuyahoga was so combustible that a spark from a passing train ignited a fire that floated downstream, charring a railroad bridge. It was said that the toxins did not just kill the river's wildlife, but mutated them. There were stories of three-eyed trout and hermaphroditic carp that carried both eggs and milt. As the river became packed with industrial waste, it barely qualified as water anymore, so a clever fish decided that if he couldn't beat the factories, he would join them. Born with abnormally long flippers and a pair of lungs, the fish crawled out of the river and presented himself at the employment office of the Jones and Laughlin Steel Company, wearing a hard hat to conceal the fact that he had no hair or ears. Giving his name as Norbert Bass, he was hired as a stoker, shoveling ore into the furnace on the night shift. The fish worked his way up to inspector, earning enough money to buy a house in Parma and a vacation timeshare in Florida. Sadly, his success led to his demise. A freshwater fish, he died while swimming in the Gulf of Mexico with his wife and children.

The Lake Erie Monster began her life as a sturgeon, hatched off Edgewater Beach. She was ten feet long, longer than most of her species.

One day, she was sucking worms out of the mud near the mouth of the Cuyahoga when she inhaled a mouthful of iron sulfite, which had floated downstream from a steel mill and settled in the riverbed. Right away, she felt a change in her body. Her snout and tail grew longer. Her fins lost their fanlike shape, becoming long, thin tentacles. Rather than a sturgeon's usual diet of insect larvae and worms, she developed a ravenous appetite for toxic waste. And in those days, the mouth of the Cuyahoga offered plenty: ferrous sulfate and fleece dust, gasoline and oil, calcium sulfate and iron scale. The monster scarfed it all. She couldn't control herself. And the more she ate, the larger and more grotesque she grew. Schools of sturgeon in which she had once swum anonymously now scattered at the sight of her, fearing she was a predator. She tried eating worms again, hoping they would restore her to the shape of a sturgeon, but she could no longer digest them. Her metabolism had changed, and now she could only consume toxins.

In her hideous new state, the creature developed a hatred of the humans who had polluted the lake and transformed her into a monster. She decided to take revenge on Cleveland, and the entire state of Ohio. After her attack on the *Cool Breeze*, a family of six reported seeing "a huge snakelike creature" off Cedar Point. A lakefront farmer claimed that one of his pigs had gone missing, and that the trail of a "long, thin creature, like a giant slug," led from his pigpen to the beach.

As the monster sightings multiplied, a marina owner offered a $5,000 reward to anyone who captured her alive, so she could be examined by a zoology professor from The Ohio State University. The marina owner labeled a containment pond on his property "Future Home of the Lake Erie Monster." The *Port Clinton Beacon* held a contest to name the monster, settling on South Bay Bessie—quickly shortened to just Bessie—after the Davis Besse Nuclear Power Plant, surely a symbol of humanity's capacity to mutate nature. A Cleveland wax museum displayed a portrait of the Great Lake Erie Serpent.

Bessie decided that harassing fishermen and farmers was not the way to punish the real culprit for her predicament: the industries that had fouled the Cuyahoga. To strike at them, she would have to sink one of the freighters that delivered iron ore to the steel mills. So she began lurking among lake traffic, seeking an opportunity to attack a boat. Sailors standing watch in pilothouses told of seeing a black head protruding thirty feet above the lake's surface, and a body "shaped like an eel's." But the largest freighters are a thousand feet long, so no matter how much toxic waste Bessie consumed, she never grew large enough to get a grip on a hull. Perhaps she could have crippled a ship by tangling herself in its propeller, but her self-loathing was never strong enough to drive her to suicide. She had to satisfy herself with being a specter, a sight so frightening she might drive sailors to quit the Lakes. As one wrote in a letter, "For the last three summers, we've seen one of the most terrific sea monsters in existence in different parts of the lake."

Bessie did not meet her end in a confrontation with a ship, or entangled in a serpent hunter's net. She disappeared because Cleveland was so embarrassed about the Cuyahoga catching fire it decided to clean up the river. The city built huge tunnels to store rainwater, so it wouldn't have to dump untreated sewage into the river during storms. The president of the United States signed a law prohibiting factories from dumping their wastes into rivers. The paint factory closed, as did the slaughterhouses. Some of the steel mills closed, too. When the mills shut down, fewer freighters docked in Cleveland. The Cuyahoga stopped smelling like rotten eggs. With the river's freshness restored, kayakers began paddling through downtown Cleveland, to Lake Erie. With each passing year, there was less toxic waste for Bessie to eat. Gradually, she began to shrivel. Her tentacles shrunk back into fins, until finally, she was a sturgeon again, eating larvae and worms.

Bessie only terrorized Lake Erie for a brief period during the 1970s and '80s, when Cleveland was at its most dismal and polluted. Yet her name and image live on as symbols of the city's nadir. Then she became a sturgeon again, and sturgeon don't concern themselves with the affairs of people, unless they find themselves on the end of a hook.

FOR FURTHER READING

The Oneida Creation Story, Demus Elm

The Algic Researches, Henry Rowe Schoolcraft

The Song of Hiawatha, Henry Wadsworth Longfellow

Plains Indian Mythology, Alice Marriott and Carol K. Rechlin

The Pawnee Mythology, George A. Dorsey

Legends of Le Detroit, Marie Caroline Watson Hamlin and James Valentine Campbell

Michigan Legends: Folktales and Lore from the Great Lakes State, Sheryl James

Legends of the Land of the Lakes, George Francis

The Voyageur, Grace Lee Nute

Werewolves and Will-O-the-Wisps: French Tales of Mackinac Retold, Dirk Gringhuis

Mike Fink: A Legend of the Ohio, Emerson Bennett

The Outlaws of Cave-in-Rock, Otto Arthur Rothert

Heroes, Outlaws, and Funny Fellows of American Popular Tales, Olive Beaupre Miller

Febold Feboldson: Tall Tales from the Great Plains, Paul R. Beath

Follow the Drinking Gourd, Jeanette Winter

The Refugee, or, The Narratives of Fugitive Slaves in Canada Related by Themselves, Benjamin Drew

Paul Bunyan, Esther Shepard

The Saginaw Paul Bunyan, James Stephens

Lore of the Lumber Camps, Earl Clifton Beck

Ballads and Songs of the Shanty-Boy, Franz Rickaby

Long Live the Hodag! The Life and Legacy of Eugene Simeon Shepard: 1854-1923, Kurt Daniel Kortenhof

The Hodag and Other Tales of the Logging Camps, Luke S. Kearney

The Hobo's Hornbook, George Milburn

Tall Tale America: A Legendary History of Our Humorous Heroes, Walter Blair

A Mouthful of Rivets: Women and Work in World War II, Nancy Baker Wise

The Long Ships Passing: The Story of the Great Lakes, Walter Havighurst

La Salle and the Discovery of the Great West, Francis Parkman

The American Songbag, Carl Sandburg

Chicago Haunts: Ghostlore of the Windy City, Ursula Bielski

Haunted Lakes: Great Lakes Ghost Stories, Superstitions and Sea Serpents, Frederick Stonehouse

The Lake Erie Monster, Shiner Comics